A QUICK
:30
SECONDS

Emerson Dunn Mysteries
by Roy Maynard

.38 Caliber
.22 Automatic
A Quick 30 Seconds

(more to come)

A QUICK 30 SECONDS

AN EMERSON DUNN MYSTERY

Roy Maynard

CROSSWAY BOOKS • WHEATON, ILLINOIS
A DIVISION OF GOOD NEWS PUBLISHERS

Cover illustration: Keith Stubblefield

Art Direction/Design: Mark Schramm

First printing, 1993

Printed in the United States of America

ISBN 0-89107-745-6

01		00		99		98		97		96		95		94		93	
15	14	13	12	11	10	9	8	7	6	5	4	3	2	1		

To my parents:
Thanks for never
noticing when my reading
light was on all night

1

The birds in my life are never jewel-encrusted Maltese falcons. That doesn't usually bother me; look at all the trouble the black bird caused Bogie. None of that for me, thank you very much.

That's not to say the birds in my life don't bring me my own share of grief. A good example is the bird that was brought into my life late on a mid-July afternoon — a Wednesday, as a matter of fact. The bird in question was a chicken. It was of the lifeless persuasion. My dog looked at me proudly.

"That's a dead chicken," I said.

He didn't respond — not that I expected him to. I talk to him anyway. That's a First Amendment right we all share.

"I think that's a felony," I told him. He just looked at me. I gave up.

I turned around and went back into the house, closing only the screen door. I walked to the telephone. Airborne Ranger (the aforementioned dog) seemed a little disappointed that he wasn't invited inside with his quarry.

I picked up the phone and dialed the number to my favorite detective sergeant, a prince of a guy named Bill Singer.

"Police . . . Singer here," he answered.

"Let's talk chickens," I said. "Is killing a chicken a crime in this state?"

"Dunn, what have you done now?" he asked.

"It wasn't me. I wasn't even a co-conspirator. It was my dog. He just brought home a chicken."

"Whose chicken?"

"I don't know. I suppose it must belong to the Millers, down the road. They have chickens."

"It used to be a capital offense, if memory serves," he said. "They used to shoot dogs who stole chickens. Didn't you know that?"

"How should I know that? I'm a suburbanite by heritage. I've never lived out in the country before."

"Did you let your dog out of the yard?"

"I wouldn't say 'let.' No . . . 'let' is too vague a word. I didn't 'let' him out of the yard. The gate was open, and I possibly knew it was open, but that's not exactly 'letting' him roam free. And besides, he's never gone that far before."

"You're outside city limits, but I think there's a county ordinance against letting dogs roam. From now on, keep him inside the fence. Here's what you do: go see Mr. Miller — he's a nice man, and that shotgun of his is hardly ever loaded — and apologize for your dog. Pay him what the chicken was worth . . . And for the eggs. If your dog scared any others, they might not lay for a few days."

"How do you know so much about chickens?"

"I learned how to be a cop from Andy Griffith. Anything else? I have cases to crack, you know — clues to find."

I paused. Now was as good a time as any.

"I do have one more question," I said. "A favor, really. A friend of mine is in trouble."

He must have heard something in my voice. He got serious. "Trouble? Criminal-type trouble?"

"Yeah . . . My old college roommate . . . He was arrested for something . . . Matthew M. Hall."

"DOB?"

"Huh?"

"Date of birth, Dunn . . . C'mon, keep up with me here."

"Yeah . . . Yeah." I pulled a crumpled piece of paper from my shirt pocket. When my old friend Danny had called me at work earlier that day with the news, I knew I'd need this information when I pumped Singer for facts. Danny always remembered people's birthdays.

"March 22, 1964," I said.

"I'm running him now," Singer said. I could hear the *tap-tap-tapping* of a computer keyboard. He was typing Matt's name and date of birth into the NCIC computer — the National Crime Information Center. As we waited, he asked what I knew about Matt's "trouble."

"Very little," I said. "A friend called and told me Matt had been arrested. He's out now — on bond, I guess."

"Is Matthew M. Hall a close friend?" Singer asked.

"Not really . . . Just an old college buddy."

"Good. It's good that you're not close, because it looks as if he could go away for a very long time. Federal grand jury indictment . . . RICO."

"Who's Rico?"

"RICO is a what, not a him, Dunn. Racketeer-Influenced and Corrupt Organizations. RICO statutes were set up to catch big-time crooks, mobsters and such. They're pretty serious. Let's see here . . . Indictment on RICO charges handed down by a grand jury in Dallas last week. You're right, he bonded out. I'll bet the bond was high. We're not talking about a traffic ticket here."

"What exactly did he do?"

"That will be in the indictment, not the computer file," Singer said. "I can find out with a few phone calls if it's that important to you."

"No, I'll find out soon enough. I'm going up to Dallas to see if there's anything I can do. I have a little vacation time coming to me, and I can leave Robert in charge."

"What about Remington?"

"She might go with me. I don't think she could bear to be without me for a whole weekend."

"I'm misting up here, Emerson. Stop it before I begin to blubber. You know what a romantic I am."

"Yeah, I know. I'd better take care of this chicken thing. Thanks for the information — on both cases."

I hung up the telephone. I looked through the screen door at my dog; he still held his trophy in his mouth. I wondered how I was going to convince him to let me have it.

"Gimme the chicken," I tried as I opened the screen door.

His tail started wagging. I walked back out to the porch and reached down to scratch his ears. He liked that.

"That's right, I'm saying nice things to you and I'm scratching your ears — so gimme the chicken."

He dropped the chicken.

"I knew it," I said. "You do speak English."

He licked me. I tried not to think about the fact that he'd just been holding a dead chicken in his mouth. I tried not to think about the chicken at all as I picked it up by its neck. I figured it was a little late to check for vital signs. I stood up and held the chicken behind my back; if Airborne couldn't see it, maybe he would forget about it.

"Go inside now," I said. I opened the screen door, and he marched into the house. I closed both doors. In a few minutes he would realize he'd been tricked. It's probably not sporting to use my superior intellect to fool an inferior species, but I was willing to live with the guilt.

I sighed and started down the porch steps. Being a parent isn't easy. I walked by my car and for a moment I thought about driving down the road to the Millers' house, but then I thought better of it; where would I put the chicken?

It took about five minutes to walk the quarter-mile or so to my neighbors' home. It was a warm, muggy afternoon — a good day to be out sailing. But I wasn't sailing. I was trying to save my dog from the death penalty.

I lived out on an obscure, unattended, and uncrowded farm-to-market road. Now that I was editor of the local paper in this small Texas Gulf Coast town, I could afford a home with an actual yard. My home was an old farmhouse, newly renovated. The farm's original acreage was leased out to a rancher who ran some cattle on it, so my only neighbors (besides the cows) were the Millers, on their own farm, just down the road.

The Millers' house was set back about twenty-five yards from the road. It was an old frame house, probably built by Mr. Miller himself. The only vestiges left of Mr. Miller's small farm were a few Black Angus cows . . . and a few chickens. Fewer chickens now.

I knocked on the faded brown door. Mrs. Miller answered; she wore a flower-print dress and a sweater, despite the heat. She was probably about seventy-five, I knew, but she was energetic and opinionated. She smiled when she recognized me.

"Emerson Dunn, how are you this evening?" she said.

"Fine, ma'am," I said. "Well, not really fine. It's this chicken . . . I think it's yours."

I held out the chicken for her to examine. She dug some reading glasses out of her sweater pocket and put them on, then bent down to get a closer look at the chicken.

"Yes, I guess it was," she said.

"My dog brought it home."

"I see." She peered at it again.

"I'm sorry," I said. "I'll reimburse you for the chicken, but I don't think we should shoot my dog. He didn't know any better. He's never lived on a farm."

"Shoot him? What are you talking about? It was only a chicken, Emerson."

"I don't have to shoot him?"

"Why should we shoot him? He was only being a dog. Now,

long ago, when the livestock and poultry were our livelihood, Mr. Miller might have been a little angry. But no one wants to shoot your dog, Emerson."

"Thank you. How much do I owe you?"

"Don't be silly, Emerson. We've got more chickens than I can care for. I'd give *you* money to take the whole flock of them home with you, if Mr. Miller didn't enjoy his fresh eggs so much. Now tell me about you. How are you doing?"

"Fine, ma'am."

"And how is work going? I read your editorial about the water bills getting too high. I agree — it's just like a tax increase if they're taking money from the water bills to pay for other things. It's sneaky, if you ask me. Now, how is your lovely fiancée?"

I took a deep breath and suppressed a grin. "Work is going fine, and she's not my fiancée, really. We're just dating."

"You two are such a nice couple. What's her name again? I've only met her once, and it usually takes me two or three times before I remember; but once I do, I remember for life."

I smiled. "It's Remington . . . I mean A. C. Remington. When I first met her I called her by her last name, and it's gotten to be a habit. Her full name is Aggie Catherine Remington."

"Such a pretty girl."

"I think so, too," I said. She smiled at me.

"Now, Emerson, give me that chicken, and I'll have Mr. Miller dispose of it. He'll do it as soon as he gets back from town. If you tried to bury it at your place, it might lead your dog into temptation."

"Yes, ma'am." I handed her the chicken. I was a little relieved; I'd been wondering what to do with it.

"Now don't be a stranger, Emerson," Mrs. Miller said. "Take care."

"Yes, ma'am, and thanks," I said.

"Bye, now."

I said good-bye as she closed the door. I walked back to my house and stopped to rinse off my hands at the hose before I went inside. When I went in, Airborne was looking at me with a hint of confusion in his eyes.

"It's gone," I said. "You've just experienced grace . . . mercy. It's a wonderful thing. Remember this."

I walked back to my kitchen. The only major appliance the house lacked was a dishwasher, so my sink was a little full. I had decided it would be best to ignore the dishes as long as they ignored me. I crossed the aging tile floor to my refrigerator (an old rounded model, probably circa 1965). I opened it slowly, standing to one side (just in case) and, after I determined it was safe, assessed the contents. Enough for a decent meal for two. I reached for the phone and dialed.

"City desk." The voice was male.

"A. C. Remington, please."

"One moment."

"A. C. Remington . . . Can I help you?"

"I hope so," I answered. "I have this sudden urge to burn things. Since arson is a felony, I decided I'd better vent my urge on a couple of steaks. Can I interest you?"

"I suppose so," she said. "I think I should encourage this new habit of yours. This is the third night this week you've barbecued for me. You're not getting tired of it?"

"Never. My parents always barbecued in the summer. My mother said it was because she didn't want to heat up the house with the oven, but I figured it was really because my dad was the better cook of the two and Mom knew it."

"You shouldn't say that about your mother."

"It's true. The poor woman means well, but she'll be in the middle of an Agatha Christie novel and forget all about what's in the oven. Besides, barbecuing is in the Dunn men's genes. I have inherited my forefathers' talents."

"We'll see. I'll be there about 7:00."

"Drive safely."

I hung up and went out to light the gas grill. The grill was a housewarming present from my friends David and Ruth. I'd used it almost every night since I'd gotten it. I fired it up and went inside to marinate the steaks for a few minutes.

I mixed up a bowlful of Super Secret Dunn Magic Marinade, With Many Mysterious Ingredients, Some Of Which Are Found In Nature, and let the steaks soak.

I knew the menu was missing certain items from the Four Basic Food Colors, such as green and yellow. I found a can of green beans with a lot of yellow on the label, so I figured it could count as both. I learned all about the Four Basic Food Colors in elementary school — in third grade, I believe. That had been a rocky year for me. I'm amazed I retained anything I learned then. There was that embarrassing incident with the paste. Kevin McAllen was probably still in therapy over that one. But we all learned something from it, and somehow I emerged from the experience with a full working knowledge of the Four Basic Food Colors (brown, green, yellow and orange/red). My life is better for it, I'm sure.

Once the beans were simmering, I rescinded my earlier decision on the dishes, since Remington was coming. I cleared out the sink — mostly, at least. Then I poured myself a Coke and went out on the back porch to sit with Airborne for a while. I wasn't really mad at him, since he was a golden retriever and all he'd done was retrieve a bird. Besides, it was mostly my fault, since I hadn't closed the gate. I broke down and scratched his ears some.

"We won't mention this to Remington," I said. "She's a little squeamish."

He seemed to concur; at least, he offered no objections.

The breeze was nice, and the sounds were relaxing. The engines of farm trucks and cars heading home rumbled low in the distance, and the high end of the musical scale was provided by birds and crickets. It was almost relaxing enough to make me forget such things as federal grand jury indictments.

Luckily the telephone rang, and when I answered, a voice on the other end brought me to reality.

"Emerson, have you decided?"

"Yes, Danny, I'll come up," I said. "But I doubt there's much I can do."

"We'd all feel better if you were here just the same. He *couldn't* have done what they've said."

"Since you brought it up, what *have* they said? You told me simple embezzlement charges. I found out a little while ago he's being busted on organized crime statutes."

"Really? All I know is what Julie told me. She said . . ."

Danny paused. I knew why.

"So Julie is involved?"

"Not with the charges . . . but with Matt. For a few months now. Almost a year, I guess."

"I see." I let out a breath. This was getting more and more complicated. "So tell me what she's told you," I said patiently.

"Well, you know . . . just that he was arrested for taking money from the church."

"How?"

"He volunteered one morning each week to do the church's books. Monday mornings. He'd sort out the offerings, then make the deposit. Twice a month he made out the paychecks for the pastor and the part-time secretary."

"He had unsupervised access to the money, then."

"Don't say it like that. You know he didn't do it."

"Tell me what he didn't do."

"They said he took some money each week and put it in a separate account — for some missionary. But the board of deacons had never heard of the missionary. Emerson, it's just got to be an error of some kind."

"Julie told you all of this."

"Yes. Matt won't talk; his lawyer told him not to."

"Does he have a good lawyer?" I asked.

"I think so. He's Julie's father."

"Hmmm."

"When will you come up?"

"I'll talk to Remington tonight. This complicates things. She'll be interested to know that Julie is involved."

"I should have told you sooner . . . Matt needs your help."

"What can I do? He has a good attorney."

"You can find out why he's considering pleading guilty."

Again I was silent.

"That's something else you hadn't told me."

"I just found out. Julie is worried."

"But you're convinced Matt didn't do it."

"Yes. And you should be, too."

"I don't know . . . I'll have to talk to Remington. I'll call you later tonight. Now, before I hang up, is there anything else you haven't told me?"

"They're engaged."

"Fine. Is that it?"

"Yes."

When I hung up I looked at the steaks marinating in a large mixing bowl. I picked up the bowl and went out onto the back porch. I used bacon tongs to gently lay the steaks on the grill. Airborne looked up at the grill with some interest.

"Dream on," I said.

He wasn't fooled. He knew he'd get the leftovers.

About thirty minutes later Remington arrived. I was sitting in a beat-up rocking chair near the grill. I heard her Volvo as it approached, so I got up and met her at the front door.

"You look great," I said. It was a true statement, if not an elaborate one. Her long brown hair was pulled back at the sides, and she wore a cool-looking white cotton oxford shirt with navy-blue pants. Her eyes were a different shade of blue altogether. I usually tried to spend large portions of my evenings looking at those eyes.

She kissed me and invited herself into the house.

"Where's Airborne?"

"Outside, ever vigilant, guarding the steaks from kitties and bunnies. Dinner is ready when you are."

"I'm starved."

We ate at the kitchen table, talking about nothing very important. When we were finished, Remington washed the dishes and I dried. It was so domestic and comfortable, it almost made me want to change my name and move out of the state.

When we were done, I followed Remington into the living room. She sat on the end of the couch (an almost-new blue four-seater), and I walked over to the bookcase on the northeast wall of the room, the one to the right of the old wood-burning stove. I found a baseball stuffed between two books on theology. I tossed the ball to Remington.

"You're not supposed to throw things in the house," she said, catching the ball with one hand. Not bad.

"I always wondered what would happen if I did."

"Terrible things." She tossed the ball back, a little faster than I'd thrown it to her. It was a little low, so I had to bend to grab it.

"At least let's do this right," I said. I held on to the ball and walked over to the coat closet, just to the left of the front door. I found my glove and another glove Remington used when she was here (or when we were embarrassing ourselves at a church softball game). I tossed her the glove, then sat down in the rocker to the left of the wood-burning stove, facing Remington. I threw her the ball. *Thunk.* Clean catch.

"So what's on your mind?" she asked, tossing the ball.

I caught it at about shoulder level. She'd thrown underhand, but a hard underhand.

"Julie," I said. I sent the ball back overhand but lightly, giving it a little bit of an arch. The farmhouse had nice, high ceilings. Probably not built for playing catch indoors, though.

"What about her?" Remington caught it without taking her eyes off me. She sounded calm, but the ball came back overhand and straight.

"Well, I think I'll probably be running into her again," I said. I held on to the ball for a moment. "She's engaged to Matt now. Danny told me earlier this evening."

I threw a breaking ball. It didn't actually break or curve at all, so Remington caught it solidly. Few sounds in this world are as honest as a baseball hitting a leather glove or a wooden bat.

"I see," she said. "Do you still want me to go up to Dallas with you?"

She sent a line drive back to the mound that I barely caught. She was keeping her elbow up nicely, following through. She had some velocity and a sort of wavering control of the ball. I threw my curve ball next. It didn't curve. "It's your decision. Would you be comfortable around her?"

She sent me a slider that had me diving off the rocking chair to catch it.

"No. You used to be in love with her. You used to be engaged to her."

I was hoping to tone things down, so I sent the ball back to her underhanded. "Then don't go," I said. "I'll go alone."

If I'd been less attentive, I'd have caught the ball in the face. Instead, I ducked, and it hit the bookcase behind me, slamming into a brass-and-glass lantern allegedly from an old sailboat. It broke the glass and ricocheted downward. I deftly deflected it with my head but caught it on the second bounce. "Wrong answer?" I asked.

"Wild pitch," she said with no remorse. "Sorry."

Again I sent the ball back to her underhanded. "Maybe Mom was right about not throwing things in the house."

"You're a grown-up now. You can do what you want. You can throw the ball in the house, you can eat dessert before dinner, you can go to Dallas by yourself."

She got a good split-fingered grip on the ball and went into her windup, which was not a simple thing to do because she was still sitting. It was a straight pitch, right in the strike zone. I caught it this time, then tossed it back.

"Tell me something," I said. "If you were me, what would you do?"

"I'd use my whole torso to throw the ball," she said. "You're pushing it away from your body. You're tall, and you've got good reach . . . Think of your body as a slingshot. Don't throw like this . . ."

She demonstrated the sort of weak, elbow-down pitch I had allegedly been making. It was the first catch I made that didn't send the rocker back a good foot or so.

"I get your point," I said, winding up. I sent her my heater, but I was a little discouraged that her expression didn't change when she caught it. No howls of pain, no immediate phone calls to major-league scouts. "But about the trip to Dallas . . ." I added.

"I was going to tell you tonight I can't go."

She held on to the ball for a minute, giving me an innocent smile.

"Then why are you mad at me?"

"You didn't come up with the right answer."

I caught the ball with my glove in my gut. I lost a little air in the maneuver. "Can I still go?"

"You're a grown-up now," she repeated. "You can do what you want. I'll still be here when you get back. I know you're over Julie. I don't think she's much competition, anyway. She probably throws like a girl."

After we cleaned up the glass from the lantern, we let Airborne in. He immediately took a position on the couch next to Remington and eyed her lovingly. I think it was mutual. She scratched his ears without being asked. She never scratched mine, even when I *did* ask.

After another hour of fairly tame discussion, we agreed that I'd leave on Saturday and stay the week.

"All I'll do is stand around being moral support," I said. "There's not much else I *can* do, as far as I can see."

"Just as long as it's not Julie you're supporting — at least not in a physical sense."

"You know what I mean. It sounds like Matt's going to plead out. First offense — a nonviolent crime. If he's nice, they might just give him probation and let him pay the money back over several years."

"Did he do it?"

"Probably. The Feds aren't going to take something they don't consider solid to the grand jury. Danny would be furious if he heard me say that. He just doesn't understand that things are usually that simple."

"Tell me more about Danny."

"He's a little naive, I guess. Raised in a churchgoing house-hold; went to a Christian school and then to the Christian college. Nice guy. He's been working for a few years now to save enough money to go to seminary. He wants to be a missionary. Like I said, a nice guy. He did kiss his prom date good night, though."

"How do you know that?"

"He told me. He said he used to feel guilty about it, until he met me. He said he probably wouldn't feel very guilty ever again, now that he knows me. I think I threw something at him when he said that."

"What about the other one?"

"The other one?"

"Weren't there four roommates in the house? You, Matt, Danny, and some other guy?"

"Yeah. The fourth guy was Pete Yates. Musician. Drummer, to be exact. I saw him around campus, and one day I asked him to write a music column for the college newspaper. It turned out to be our most popular feature. Pete was the main reason we all moved out of the dorm our senior year. He'd joined a band, and he needed to practice. They frown on late-night drum practice in the dorms, even if you stuff towels in the drums. Matt came up with this deal on the house we rented, and Pete took over the garage for his drums and his practicing. We didn't mind it."

"You've talked about him."

"Some. I liked him a lot. He's still in Dallas, playing in some of the clubs there. When his band makes it down to Houston, I usually go. I took David and Ruth with me once."

"What's the name of the band?"

"Sergeant Marvel. The reference is reportedly to Captain Marvel's underachieving younger brother."

"Are they any good?"

"Sure," I said after a pause. What did I know about musical talent? Not much. But they sure seemed to get good press whenever any of the small music magazines in Texas wrote about them.

"Where will you stay in Dallas?"

"With Mom and Dad, I guess. Or maybe with Danny."

"You'll enjoy that. Who's going to run the newspaper?"

"Robert."

"Good. He'll do a good job."

"Yeah. He's young, he's talented, he's good-looking, he's personable, and he's got a good grasp of how to do my job. I hope the IRS audits him."

"You're talented, good-looking, and personable, too," Remington said. "You were young once, but let's not dwell on the past."

I nodded. I was slated to turn thirty later that year; Remington was four years younger than me. Still, Airborne was about thirty-five in dog-years, so I didn't feel so bad. Except when he pointed out that I was going to be 210 in dog-years.

Remington left at about 10 P.M.; she had to get up and go to work in the morning. I did, too. I went to bed after the news. Airborne was taking up more than his half of the bed, but I didn't kick him off.

I thought about Aggie Catherine Remington. Remington and I had been dating about six months or so, and things were starting to look serious. Everyone, including my best friend David, expected me to pop The Question any day now. I was stalling. I wasn't sure why.

Maybe it was Julie. Maybe there were still some feelings I had to figure out before I was ready to commit to Remington.

Or maybe it was just shameless fear. My money was on fear.

Airborne let out a doggie sigh. At least *he* found it easy to sleep. I thought more about Julie.

We'd met in an art class. That was her major; I just needed an extra class. I sat on the back row, usually with my shirt untucked. And that was the semester I wore sunglasses for four months. My regular glasses had broken, but my prescription sunglasses worked just fine. One of the girls in that class had asked me why I always wore them. I told her it was to hide my drug problem, my bloodshot eyes. I think she believed me. She didn't speak to me for the rest of the semester.

Julie spoke to me. She gradually drifted back a few rows and eventually sat against the wall with me. The professor knew we were both fairly reliable. We'd both show up prepared, and usually at least one of us would have an opinion on the work of whatever Dead Guy Painter we were studying.

Then one day she asked me out. Being a modern sort of guy, I only stuttered for a moment before accepting. She was pretty, smart, and a little out of place on the campus of the Christian college because she was, well, allegedly a little wild.

Skip the allegedly. After that first date, I figured it was meant to be. I was new to the whole religion thing, and her brand of it was far less imposing than most. She relied fairly heavily on grace, and I think she considered sanctification an option. Our activities were fairly tame by the world's standards, but scandalous on that conservative campus. For over a year we dated, spending time at restaurants and pubs, coming back to the dorms too late to escape notice. Then we were engaged. The plan was for me to graduate, get a job, and wait for her to graduate the next year. I did my part, but after working for a few months I got a call from Julie. She'd started dating someone else, someone local, someone she could see more than once a month. I said fine, keep the ring. She said she'd send it back. It came by United Parcel Service a few days later.

It was months before I dated again. But a recent set of circumstances, involving a political candidate and corruption in the police department, caused me to spend a good deal of time with one Aggie Catherine Remington, my current love-pumpkin.

I fell asleep thinking of the bodily harm A. C. Remington would cause to my body if she ever heard me refer to her as "my current love-pumpkin."

My phone rang before my alarm clock did. The clock said 7:20; the phone said, "Are you asleep?"

"Yes," I replied (to the phone, not the alarm clock). "Will that stop you?"

"No," David said in a thick Mediterranean accent. "Let's have breakfast. We need to talk. I got a call from Israel."

"Wanda's in an hour?"

"Good. Thanks."

I hung up and assessed my surroundings. Airborne was on the cool hardwood floor now, looking at me with a little bit of curiosity.

"Dave needs to talk," I said. "Don't worry, I'll feed you first."

David, my photographer, had sounded a little upset. And David was a hard guy to upset. It must have been something pretty important. David, a native Israeli, had been in the Israeli Defense Forces during the 1982 invasion of Lebanon. Somewhere along the way he'd developed a detached calmness as suited to a photographer as to a tank commander. Before joining his mother in America after college, David had been a freelance photographer, shooting riot scenes on the West Bank and the Gaza Strip. He had walked into my newspaper office about two years earlier, a few days after arriving in America. We hired him on the spot after seeing his portfolio. Not a bad decision.

I let Airborne out, and then I showered and got dressed. When I finished, he was ready to come in and eat. I pulled out a bag of diet doggie food — embarrassing, I know, but what else can you do with a fat golden retriever? — and filled his bowl. He stopped eating long enough to walk me to the door. He was probably hoping he could go with me.

"No, you stay here," I said. "Protect the homestead from bunnies."

Ten minutes later I pulled into our favorite breakfast place, Wanda's Truck Stop. David was already inside. I sat down facing him in the booth.

"What's up?" I asked.

"I got a call last night . . . Israel . . . My gunner . . ."

"From the army?"

"Yeah. We went through tank school together. He was a good gunner. He died two days ago . . . his back."

"I don't understand."

"Shrapnel. We were in position on the outskirts of Beirut. I was commanding the tank. The crew wanted to get out, stretch their legs. I said yes, but I stayed on the tank. A few minutes later a mortar shell lands nearby. Gershom takes shrapnel in the spine . . . high up. He was crippled, and it got worse. The shrapnel was too close to his spinal cord for them to remove all of the pieces. He died two days ago, even though it happened so many years ago."

I nodded. I could see in David's eyes that there was more. He looked down into his coffee cup. His hands were tense around it.

"It would be impossible to stay in the tank twenty-four hours a day," he said. "But it was still my decision. I let them go out. My instincts said no; we could have waited. It was only an hour until dark. But my judgment said, 'why not?' I went with my judgment."

"Who called from Israel?"

"His father. He doesn't blame me."

"But you do."

"I do."

A waitress came, bringing me some coffee, and we ordered. "Does Ruth know?" I asked. Ruth was David's girlfriend. She grew up in a nice, stable Jewish home in Houston near Rice University. She loved David, but according to Remington, she didn't always understand him.

"No," David replied. "I should tell her?"

"If you want," I said after a moment. "It might help. It might help her, too. She doesn't understand much about the war. You spent eighteen months in combat; you were in one of the first tanks over the border during the invasion of Lebanon. Then you patrolled the Golan Heights for a few more months, dodging the occasional Syrian shell. Ruth spent those years in high school in Houston. What does she know about war?"

"She shouldn't want to know anything about it."

"But she wants to know more about you. She told Remington that. She feels like she doesn't know much about why you're the way you are. She doesn't know your background."

"You should talk. What does Remington know about you?"

"You're changing the subject."

"Are you still going to Dallas? And taking Remington?"

"No . . . I mean, yes . . . I mean, I'm still going to Dallas, but I'm not taking Remington. There have been some complications. Luckily, Remington couldn't get off work anyway."

"Complications?"

"Julie," I said. "She's engaged to the guy I'm supposed to help."

"She seems to get engaged a lot."

"Only twice," I said. "To me and then him. I didn't ask about details, but knowing Matt I would expect they've been going out for quite a while if he's asked her to marry him. She probably started dating him when she dumped me."

"It doesn't still bother you, does it? It shouldn't. You've been dumped by better girls than her. A lot of them."

"Who asked you?"

"Just trying to help," he said with a grin.

Now that the mood had lightened up a bit (talking about our floundering love lives always lightened the mood), I brought the conversation back around to Gershom.

"Will you go to the funeral?"

He shook his head. "It's today."

"David, I can't help you much. I can't tell you it's all right, that it wasn't your fault. But Mordechai knows military procedure. And you respect his opinion. Have you talked to him yet? And if he told you it's okay, would you believe him?"

"He's already said that. He said the unit was at a stepped-down level of alert, that I was right to let the men stretch their legs."

Mordechai, David's uncle, had come to the States a few weeks ago and had already bought a business (and helped us through a bit of nasty business we'd run into ourselves). He was living with his sister Rebecca (David's mother), her husband Carl, and David. Carl, an American oil engineer, enjoyed having the large, bearded Israeli around during times of great crisis, such as whenever Rebecca decided she didn't approve of whatever they were doing. The two older men took some of the scrutiny off David and me, though Rebecca was still convinced her purpose in life was to make the two of us into acceptable husband material for Ruth and Remington.

Unfortunately, we weren't doing much to cooperate with her. For one thing, despite her best efforts we hadn't given up cigars completely. About once a month we'd sit on David's back porch and do our part to kill mosquitoes, and now that I'd moved into the farmhouse, we'd fumigated my backyard as well.

David and I finished our breakfasts.

"Will you need any help?" he asked as I downed the last of my coffee.

I put my cup down and shook my head. "I don't think so. How bad could it be? I'll go up, ask a few questions, and tell everybody that they should leave it to the court system now. I'm half-convinced Matt is guilty, anyway."

"Sherri is getting pretty good in the darkroom. And I have a lot of vacation time saved. You need me, you call. Or even just page me. I can be at your parents' house or anywhere else in Dallas in five hours. Two if I fly."

"Thanks."

We left Wanda's and went to the newspaper office. Thursday was a light day for the editor (me) but not for everyone else. The reporters, Sherri and Robert, had to write their stories so I'd have something to edit Friday morning. Friday afternoon we put the Sunday paper together; my plan was to leave at about 7 P.M. Friday from the office, thereby getting the paper out the door and avoiding the downtown Houston traffic on my way north to Dallas.

"Hi, chief," Sherri said as I walked into the office and went to my desk. While I didn't have an office, I did have an executive desk. That meant there was room not only for Mr. Potato Head, but also for less important things such as my computer terminal and notepads.

Robert, the other reporter, wasn't in the office yet, and it looked as if Louise, the publisher, was still out. Her office was dark. But Sharon, the receptionist, was on the phone. She waved as I passed. I looked for those dangerous pink message slips on my desk and found none. I turned my attention back to Sherri.

"Hello, Sherri. Been out terrorizing the school board lately?" I asked.

"Yup. I should get banner placement. Remember that outside audit the board approved Tuesday night? That's not unusual, because they have to have one once a year. But I kinda thought it was a weird time for it, in July. So I started poking around. It appears they're going to sack a money-man — but they'll all call it a resignation."

My day was getting brighter. "Mitchell?"

"No, not the assistant superintendent for finance. One of his assistant assistant supers. Some guy named Bose. He never came out of his office much, so I didn't know him other than by sight."

"Does the district suspect criminal activity?"

"They're denying it so hard that they must."

"Good. Don't nail the guy to the wall yet, though. We'll let the auditor do that. At this point let's just stick to the fact that he's resigning at the same time they're bringing in someone to audit the books. Focus on the instability."

She looked at me with a hint of disbelief in her expression. "Chief? . . . Is that you? Mr. 'Let's Nail The Slimebags'? This is possible misuse of public funds!"

"That's unfair," I said. "Have I ever used the word 'slime-bags'?"

"Yes."

"Oh, yeah. Never mind what I just said. Get 'em. Find a source to admit suspicion first, though. The head of the teachers' union should be good for that. She always keeps in touch with what the administration bad guys are up to."

A few minutes later Robert came in. We all had a brief story meeting and outlined the Sunday paper's contents. We then made some tentative assignments for early next week. I let Robert handle that part; he'd be filling in for me in getting out next week's papers, both the Thursday and Sunday editions.

The meeting lasted a record fourteen minutes (my average was nine). We adjourned. Specifically the reporters adjourned to their terminals, and I adjourned to the darkroom. David was processing a few rolls of film. When I knocked I heard a muffled "Come in."

"You know, I think you were right," I said as I entered the darkroom. A pan with four rolls of negatives on wire spools was being flushed with water. David was leaning against the counter, watching his film wash.

"You know," he said, "that shouldn't surprise you. You should be used to it by now."

"As I was saying, I think those guys could handle the paper just fine without us."

"So you want me to come?"

"No, not yet. I might not be up there more than a day or so. But if it looks like I need you, I'll call. Hey, maybe we can catch a Rangers game."

David grinned. Ruth and I had taken him to his first baseball game a year ago, before I started dating Remington. He seemed to enjoy the part where you call the umpire names. And although the Texas Rangers were, for the most part, little more than mediocre, they were *our team*.

"That would be nice," he said. "Think they'll kick us out of the stadium again?"

F riday evening I left the newspaper office by 6:30 and headed north for Dallas. Remington was going to take care of Airborne for me. I told her she only needed to stop by a couple of times a day, but she said she'd stay at the house while I was away so the poor mutt wouldn't be lonely at night.

I stopped for gas in Huntsville and again in Ennis. By 11:15 I was on the outskirts of Dallas, heading east on Interstate 20. I had decided to stay with Danny instead of with my parents, just for the sake of convenience. At about ten minutes to midnight I pulled into a parking lot in front of an apartment complex just north of Mesquite, a suburb of Dallas. I got out, grabbed my bag, and walked up the stairs to Danny's apartment.

He had lived in the same place since we'd graduated. After graduation he started working the sound system at First Baptist Church. With the three services on Sunday and the numerous other functions throughout the week, it was a full-time job. It paid enough for Danny to live in a relatively safe neighborhood and save a little money every month. He planned to go to seminary in a year or so.

The apartment complex was one in a sea of condos, apartments, and townhomes (only real estate agents really know the difference between the three). The sea stretched for miles and miles east along Interstate 30, the product of too-optimistic developers and irresponsible bankers in the 1980s. Many units were never occupied. Now the thousands of apartments were in varying degrees of disrepair. Danny's complex was fairly well maintained, but it didn't have long. Within fifteen years the place would be razed and something else, probably equally useless, would be built.

I hit the buzzer beside his second-floor apartment's door. A moment later I heard the deadbolt sliding back.

Danny didn't say anything; he just stepped back to allow me in. He looked terrible.

"You look terrible," I said astutely.

"Thanks. It's been a long week."

Danny was a couple of inches taller than me, which put him at about 6'1". He didn't weigh much more, so we both fit the "slim" category. We preferred to think of it in terms of the Jimmy Stewart Build. Except Jimmy Stewart was even taller, and he got the girl in almost every one of his movies. Danny and I never got the girl. We went to the Homecoming game with each other.

His usually bright eyes looked weary. It wasn't fatigue. I'd been through enough all-nighters with the guy to know when he was tired and when he was bone-deep weary. I dropped my bag in a corner of the small apartment and sat down at the even smaller kitchen table.

"Get us both a root brewski," I said. "And tell me about it."

Danny complied.

"You'll have to go through Julie's dad," he said as he sat down, handing me a bottle. Neither of us used a glass. "Matt isn't supposed to talk to anyone about the case."

"I'll call Julie's dad tomorrow."

"I've already done that. We'll drive over at 9 in the morning."

"His office?"

"Yeah. Matt won't be there."

"Fine. Just what did you tell the venerable A. Vernon Robbins my role in this is?"

"He's the one who asked for you."

I contemplated this as I emptied the bottle. I'd always gotten the impression that A. Vernon Robbins, Julie's father, probably thought his baby girl could do better than me. If pressed, I'd probably have to agree with him. Vernon specialized in defending the doctors in medical malpractice cases, so I wondered why he was taking on a criminal case — a federal criminal case, no less. As a favor to his daughter, because Matt was broke? I figured I'd better ask A. Vernon directly, so I let it pass for now.

"Danny, what if Matt's guilty?"

"He's not. He couldn't be."

"Okay. I didn't think I'd get anywhere with that one."

"What's that mean?"

"I wish I was as confident as you, that's all."

That pretty much killed the conversation. Danny announced that we had an early morning appointment to keep, so we'd better get some sleep. I agreed and stretched out on the couch after washing up. I'd been on this couch before, but under less depressing circumstances. I fell asleep thinking about Matt, wondering if he was guilty and why Danny was so sure he wasn't.

In the morning Danny offered to make some breakfast. I said a bagel would do fine and took a shower. A few minutes later we were in his truck heading west on I-30 into downtown Dallas. Julie's dad had an office in the Texas Commerce Bank Tower. It took about thirty minutes to get there and find an open parking place. We walked through the glass doorways of the huge structure, past a security desk, and over to the elevators. We found one going in the right direction. It had been a few years, so I didn't remember the floor. Danny reached over and hit the button for the 24th floor. A few moments later the doors slid open, and we walked out into a foyer. Now I remembered. Danny followed me to the left, and we walked past several doors with small brass plates on them, denoting what businesses they fronted. A few doors down on the right we found A. *Vernon Robbins, Attorney-at-law*. I'd never found out what the A. stood for. I tried the door; it was, obviously, unlocked.

"Danny, the last time I went through this door it was to tell the old guy I was going to marry his daughter. What am I doing now?"

"Saving his future son-in-law," Danny said. "Go on."

"Saving him? What can I possibly do? Tell the Feds he's a nice guy and that he helped me with my tax forms?"

"Go on."

I went in. The blue pile carpet was about five years out of date but well-maintained. The furnishings were in dark blue leather. The pictures were calming prints of forest scenes, with dark wood frames. A few brass items added a low, understated luster to the office. Only the receptionist's desk was in this front waiting room. It was directly in front of the entrance, and to the left of it was the door leading to the inner offices. That door was open.

"Mr. Robbins?" Danny called.

"In here, boys."

I remembered the voice. Smug. He was about to ask me for help, and he'd do it while calling me "son" and "my boy." I had often had the urge to counter his references by calling him "Dad." I wonder how that would have gone over. It even made my *real* dad nervous when I did that.

We walked into A. Vernon's office. It was wall-to-wall bookshelves with a few paintings — originals, I'm sure — and more than a few brass knickknacks. I'm not exactly sure what a knickknack is, but I'm quite positive the world has altogether too many of them — and that a good percentage of them were in A. Vernon Robbins's office.

The only thing I really liked about his office was his globe.

He had a globe the size of a beach ball on an elegant wooden stand in the corner. It was dusty and out of date, but I still liked it.

A. Vernon was seated behind his desk. His desk was clear. He'd learned long ago to let his paralegals and secretaries handle his paperwork for him. About all he did was sign things, talk into his Dictaphone, and do depositions in a conference room next-door. He didn't deal with much paper. He said that was the secret to efficiency. I didn't doubt him.

"Good to see you, Emerson. You look well."

"You too," I said honestly. He was in his mid-fifties, trim, with salt-and-pepper hair and a strong handshake. He wore a suit and those half-glasses he used for reading. He usually didn't bother to take them off when he wasn't reading.

He motioned to the leather chairs in front of his desk. Danny and I sat down.

"Matthew is low on funds," the lawyer said. "That's why I called you. That's why I've taken his case, in fact."

That answered that.

"I have a list of the charges," he continued. "And I have a telephone number for the prosecutor from the U.S. attorney's office. But not much else. I have almost no cooperation from my client. What I need is to have some digging done. Out of respect for my daughter, I can't — won't — hire a private investigator to look into her boyfriend's dealings. That's what I need from you. You have the skills. You know how to chase paper, I assume. Daniel here tells me you're now an exceptional investigative reporter."

"I've never investigated my friends."

A. Vernon paused. He smiled for a moment.

"He needs you. A few days ago he asked me to change his plea from 'not guilty' to 'guilty.' He gave me no reason. He's given Julie no indication why he would want to do that."

"Perhaps because he *is* guilty?"

Danny stiffened. A. Vernon waved absently at him.

"No, Daniel, your friend is correct. That was my first, and proper, assumption. Not that it would have changed my attitude toward the boy, nor my vigor in defending him. But if the U.S. attorney says he's guilty, and he says he's guilty, who am I to argue? Still, there's a glitch. I believed him when he told me he wasn't guilty. I still do. Therefore, I have stalled him — for now."

"So what am I supposed to be doing?" I asked.

"Look for signs of guilt or innocence. Preferably innocence, since my daughter will be a difficult woman to deal with if we blow this."

I smiled. "I'll do it. I'll start by going to his church — his former church, I assume — tomorrow. Then I'll drop in on Matt."

5

Danny and I had lunch at a barbecue restaurant in the Dallas suburb of Garland. Danny seemed pleased I was now involved in Matt's defense. I don't think I was pleased much, but I didn't mention it. We talked about old schoolmates, including Greg, who had galumphed off to Taiwan for a couple of years for no apparent reason, but had come home with a wife so pretty that we forgot all about asking why he ever left Texas in the first place. We talked about Pete, who was still with the band Sergeant Marvel, and about a few others. One of our school's baseball team pitchers had spent some time with the Pittsburgh Pirates. Several more of our friends were just doing the normal, expected things: working, getting married, having kids.

We discussed our own prospects for love and marriage. Danny told me he had been dating a girl he met at church, who also wanted to attend seminary, and I brought Danny up-to-date on the Remington Situation. Namely, no, I hadn't bought any jewelry lately, and no, she hadn't dumped me.

The tension was wearing off. In retrospect, most of the tension was mine, I suppose. Danny just wanted me to listen to A. Vernon.

"How's David?" he asked as we were finishing lunch.

"Fine," I said. "He's not married either, but I think Ruth is getting a little tired of waiting for him to ask."

I dug into my wallet for money and came across the business card that had David's beeper number on it. I had the number memorized after all these months, of course, so I handed the card to Danny.

"He wouldn't mind coming up if we need him," I said. "Here's his number. It's a beeper. So if I get taken hostage by a mad church secretary during my investigation, give him a call. Or if we decide to see a Rangers game."

Danny pocketed the card. I paid for lunch.

We left the restaurant and headed for Danny's apartment. There was a message on his machine when we got back. I knew the voice. She seemed to assume that I would.

"Can you two come by my apartment? I'll be here until pretty late. Pete's band is playing tonight, down in Deep Ellum. Matt and I are going. You guys want to come? They go on at 10:00."

The message ended with a series of beeps. Danny reached for the phone and dialed seven digits. "Hi. It's me. We'll come by now." He paused. "Okay. We can do that." He hung up.

"Now?" I asked.

"No, we'll just go over early tonight. Matt is picking her up at 10:00, so she wants us to drop by at about 8:30. Her father already told her you're involved. I couldn't tell if she was happy about that or not."

"I suppose we'll find out soon enough."

Deep Ellum is the funky section of Dallas. The second to the last time I had been there, wearing what I considered casually funky garb, I was about seven generations out of style. So the last time I went I wore my standard button-down shirt and loosened tie, along with pleated pants (because I'm skinny, most of my pants are pleated) and black penny-loafers. Since it was cold and misty, I had worn my trench coat, and I think I convinced at least a couple of people that it was a new style —

Bogart-funk. But most of the rest of the people looked at me as if I were Jimmy Stewart hanging out at a punk bar. Except the girls. They didn't look at me at all.

I decided to suppress my wardrobe phobia until it was time to leave. No use in developing any extra ulcers until about 8 P.M. or so.

For the rest of the afternoon Danny and I talked about our year in the house with Matt and Pete. For the most part we had been too busy to realize that those were some pretty great times — the days we'd look back on and smile about. We'd been too keen on getting out into The Real World to realize that The Real World usually isn't as much fun as college.

We ate some dinner — frozen corndogs — at about 7:00 and started getting ready to see Julie and go out for the evening.

"So you're my date again," Danny said. "I thought we were beyond this. We even have girlfriends now, and I'm still getting dressed up to go out with you."

"It could be worse. I'm a cheap date. Not like some. Remember that girl you dated our junior year?"

"Which one?"

"What do you mean, 'Which one?' You only had one date that whole year. Remember? Hilda?"

"Her name wasn't Hilda. It was Heidi. And I may have had only one date, but it was with her *and* her roommate Laura."

"No way," I said.

"Remember? You were all moony over that girl from Palau, and you had a date with her that Friday night. You waited for her in the student lounge, and I waited with you. Heidi and Laura were there, and we asked what they were doing that night. They started complaining that no one ever asked them out, so I did. Both of them. At the same time. They said it was the nicest date they'd ever had."

"Yeah, that fits. All I remember is you asking me for an extra twenty bucks. I guess you had to feed them both."

"Wrong. *You* asked *me* for twenty bucks. You still owe it to me, too. Got it on you?"

"That's ridiculous. You'd never have loaned me twenty bucks. You knew what kind of credit risk I was."

"Oh, yeah."

I decided to ask about Julie. I hadn't seen her in a quite a while and, to be honest, I hadn't even asked about her in months.

"What's Julie doing now?"

"Well, she's working in a law office," Danny said. "She works four ten-hour days a week as a secretary. Mostly typing stuff. Her dad got her the job. She has Fridays and weekends off, so she likes it, I think. But she's also talked about looking for something else, something more interesting."

I nodded.

"And there's no telling what color her hair is, either," Danny added.

I nodded again and went back to getting ready.

After about fifteen minutes of anxiety and soul-searching, I decided to just wear some jeans and a knit shirt. No one would mistake me for funky. We drove my car to Julie's, with plans to follow her and Matt to Deep Ellum in it. If I owned anything at all that was in the least bit funky, it was that car — my sky-blue '73 Ford. At least I thought so.

Danny directed me as I drove to an apartment complex on North Dallas Parkway, a few blocks north of Loop 635, also known as LBJ Freeway. We found a parking place and went to a first-floor apartment unit with plants by the door. The plants didn't look healthy. Typical Julie.

It would, of course, be romantic to say that my heart raced when Danny knocked on the door. In truth, however, my palms sweated, and my stomach tensed. Julie opened the door. She looked better than she had in college. She was only about 5'1", but she made up in attitude what she lacked in stature. Her reddish-brown hair and simple black dress made her look just about as contemporary as it's legal to be without having your picture hung in a hair salon. The reddish hue in her hair was a new addition. On some girls, the combination of red hair and green eyes would have come off like bad Christmas decorations. On her it was *avant garde*, whatever *avant garde* means — I hoped I'd never be funky enough to know for sure.

"Come in. It's nice to see you, Emerson."

Julie — the girl to whom I was once ready to pledge my life — stood back, and we entered. I hadn't thought of a witty response to her opening line, so I stayed quiet. I figured Danny would know just what to say.

"Hello," he said.

See? I knew I had made the right choice in letting Danny do the talking. But then he nudged me.

"Hello," I said. "Your hair is red."

She laughed. "It's been red several times in the last two years. You'd be amazed at the number of other colors it's been also."

"Hmmm." That wasn't a witty response, but it was a response nonetheless.

"Danny tells me you're seeing someone."

Not even thirty seconds into the conversation and already we were into the meaty stuff. "Yup."

"What's her name?"

"That's still unresolved."

"What?"

"I call her Remington . . . her last name. Her first name is Aggie, but she hates it, so I can't call her Aggie. She goes by A. C. Remington professionally, but that's too formal. I can't go on calling her Remington forever."

"Oh?" Julie's eyebrows raised a little. Her eyebrows were sculpted by what sure appears to be a very painful process: plucking. I once bought one of those car seat covers that's made of thousands of wooden beads — you know, the kind that's supposed to massage you into a comfortable state of bliss as you drive. I used it for a total of forty minutes. It was a sunny day, and I was wearing shorts. Every time I moved, those evil beads would pluck hairs from the backs of my legs. I gave the seat cover to David. He didn't wear shorts much.

It's strange how your mind wanders when you find yourself trapped. But back to Julie's implied question.

"What was the question?" I asked ever so sincerely.

"Why shouldn't you keep calling her by her last name? Is it going to change?" Julie looked innocently curious. She was good at that.

"Not that I know of," I said.

Danny nudged me again.

"I mean, not that anything wouldn't happen that I don't know of, either." I said. I realized I was babbling, so I gave up. Julie let it pass.

"Danny has told you about me and Matt?"

"Yeah." Back to one-word answers. They're always safest. I looked around the room we'd walked into. I hadn't looked at much but Julie until then. The room was typical Julie. There was a shapeless aqua-blueish couch with poofy pillows and a black metal-and-glass coffee table. Two chairs facing the couch were also that strange aqua color I was sure I'd never seen before, and they were also formless. The carpet was such a light gray that at first I thought it was white. There were a few Monet prints on the walls. Julie loved Monet. Monet got on my nerves. Probably because I didn't ever actually pay much attention in that art class we took together. I studied enough to stay prepared, but I didn't retain much appreciation for impressionistic art. I wandered toward the prints. Above the couch was Monet's *The Bridge at Argenteuil*. I knew that was the name of it because it said so in little letters on the mat, just above the frame. It had two fuzzy sailboats. I like my sailboats a little more defined.

"I thought you'd like that one," Julie said.

"Hmm," I said, which actually wasn't a comment. I usually tried to keep from commenting about Monet. I felt myself slipping into old behavior patterns; it was probably just for lack of knowing how else to act. I shook off the feeling of complacency with that and looked at Julie.

"Tell me how much trouble Matt is in."

She paused, then sat on the couch. I sat in a chair across from her, and Danny did also. Only he sat in a different chair.

"He won't talk to me or to Dad. At first he said he didn't do what they accused him of. But now he says he wants to plead guilty."

I thought about it. Once again it was phrased just so: "he wants to plead guilty." At no point did anyone say he'd confessed. No one said Matt said, "I did it." He just wanted to plead guilty — sort of like a migrating duck who just wanted to fly low over marshes to see if any hunters were there. Obviously, I was going to have to talk to Matt himself. Almost on cue, a knock came at the door. Julie got up and let Matt in. I watched as she kissed him hello, wondering if I'd feel anything. There was a twang somewhere near my kidney, I think, but not much else.

Matt hugged her for a moment, then turned to face us. He looked as annoyingly handsome as he always had. He was trim but muscular, with short, dark hair and attentive eyes. He had a firm face, and he smiled, but it was only with his mouth. His eyes resisted the gesture.

"Hi, Matt," I said. He made no attempt to shake my hand, but he didn't look displeased to see me.

"Hello, Emerson. Danny said you were driving up. What brings you here?"

I looked at Danny. Danny looked blank. "You," I said. Back to the safe one-word answers.

"Me?"

47

"I was worried. You're in trouble."

Matt lost the smile. "Trouble . . . Yeah, I guess I am."

"What can I do to help?"

Matt looked sullen. "Let's not worry about those things tonight, okay? Let's just go see Pete."

I nodded. We left Julie's apartment in two cars. Danny and I rode in silence. Let me qualify that. It sounds literary to say, "we rode in silence," but actually I had a few rust holes in certain areas of my car that made it somewhat less than soundproof. Consequently, we rode without saying much because at 60 miles per hour we wouldn't have been able to hear each other anyway.

We took U.S. Highway 75 south for about fifteen minutes before taking a downtown exit. We crawled through a few outlying streets and eventually found ourselves on Elm, the main drag of Deep Ellum. We found a parking place in front of a furniture wholesale warehouse a few blocks down from the bars, and I gave five bucks to a guy who was sitting on a loading dock and serving as a self-appointed car guardian. He looked half-pickled, as if he would pass out before 11 P.M., but it was sort of a Deep Ellum tradition to pay these guys to watch your car.

We found Matt and Julie outside the appropriate bar, which had the name of Pete's band misspelled on its marquee. We paid a couple of bucks each to get in, and I was somewhat offended that they didn't card me. More signs of advancing age. I asked the guy at the door when Pete's band was supposed to take the stage.

"Half hour or so," he said.

Matt led as we worked our way through the crowd. We were in an old warehouse that had the typical high ceilings, glass windows up high, and a cement floor. The bar was along the wall to our left, while the stage was in the front, in the right-hand corner as we entered. The stage appeared to be just a few pieces of plywood nailed together on top of a support of some kind. The instruments were ready, including Pete's mix-and-match drum set.

Tables were interspersed throughout the establishment in strategically inconvenient places. It was impossible to walk in a straight line for long. There were probably 150 people milling around. Not a big crowd for a Saturday night, but I knew it would get more crowded around midnight. Another reason I could never be funky — I have trouble staying up that late. We found a table near the stage (but not too close to the stacked speakers) and sat down. Matt held Julie's chair for her. I'd never done that, but then, when I knew her, she'd probably have slugged me if I had. We'd been sitting for about thirty seconds when Pete walked up.

"Hey, guys," he said with a broad grin. He looked happy to see us. "I'm glad you could make it. Can I sit down?"

He knew he didn't have to ask, but then he'd always been awfully polite — especially for a guy who'd made the college administration so nervous. Pete's long hair was back in a pony-tail, and he had a cross dangling from one ear. He looked comfortable in this bar. He probably looked comfortable in just about any bar. His band was composed of solid Christians, but they didn't limit their venues to youth groups and church lock-ins. When Pete was writing the music column for me in college, he'd laid out his views: we're supposed to go out into all the world, and that probably includes funky bars where the women all wear black.

"Emerson, how was the trip?" he asked.

"Fine . . . Fast . . . How's the band?"

"Not so bad," he grinned. "We've learned a fourth note. I don't think we'll ever use it, though."

"So who needs more than three?" I grinned back.

Pete turned to Danny. "Want to do us a favor?"

Danny nodded. He did everyone favors.

"Steve's running the sound board. You'd do a better job of it. He hasn't figured out what all those knobs are for yet."

Steve was the singer; he knew a little more about electronics than the rest of the band but apparently not much. Danny said, "Sure, glad to" and went back to the table toward the rear of the bar where the sound board was resting. I watched. He barely glanced at the board before he started fiddling with the knobs. He'd wait for a sound check before doing the fine-tuning, I knew; I'd seen him work the sound at dozens of events at school and church.

A waitress came over and asked for our orders. We all ordered Cokes, and she raised an eyebrow but didn't comment. We made as much small talk as was possible through the noise for a few minutes, and then Pete got a high sign from someone near the stage. It turned out to be Steve, who changed his image more often than Julie. He waved at us, then turned back to what he was doing.

"You guys have fun," Pete said as he stood. "Don't feel as if you have to stay through the whole show on my account."

"We'll leave when we've gotten our two bucks' worth," I said.

Pete grinned and went to the stage. Steve and two other guys I didn't know as well started tuning up. They sent Danny a chord or two every so often so he could check their sound levels. The guitar player was getting a little feedback on the high end, but Danny knocked it out before they started playing.

I'd heard most of the songs before, but I still enjoyed the show. Besides, as long as they played I didn't have to talk or worry about Matt or Julie. It was a little awkward, me sitting at a table with the two of them. Danny was still at the sound board.

After about forty-five minutes, the band took a break. Matt looked a little restless and leaned over to whisper something to Julie.

"We ought to be going now," Julie said to me without having

paused long enough to think about what Matt had told her. "We're kind of tired. You guys can stay."

"I've got a better idea," I said. "Why don't you let Danny take you home, Julie? You guys can use my car. I'd like some time alone with Matt."

Matt looked uncomfortable. He stared down at his empty glass. "I can't say much," he said. "Julie's dad told me to not talk about it."

"Fine. Then we'll talk about old times."

Julie shrugged. She didn't mind my car so much. Danny came over from the sound board.

Steve and Pete came over to talk to us.

"We're going to ditch your second set," I said. "Don't take it personally. You guys are pretty good. You might want to think about using that fourth note, though."

"Yeah, thanks," Steve said. He looked a little confused. Pete stuck out his hand.

"You have my number, right?" he said as we shook.

"Yeah," I said. "I might give you a call later this week."

"Great."

Steve said he'd take over the sound again, and we left the bar. Outside the door we paused and just looked at each other. I handed my keys to Danny.

"Take care of that beautiful machine," I said. "Let's go, Matt. I'll buy you some coffee."

We parted, and I followed Matt to his car, a brand-new Pontiac. Great. Vernon, Julie's father, had told me to look out for any signs of guilt, which would include extravagance. The car wasn't a Mercedes, but it wasn't a beat-up Honda Civic either.

"Nice car," I said.

"Thanks."

We got in, and Matt started the engine. We pulled out and headed for downtown. We picked up Interstate 30 and went east, toward Danny's place. I guess Matt assumed I'd be staying with Danny.

"Tell me about it, Matt."

He didn't say anything for a while. "I guess it's over," he said eventually.

"What's over?"

"My career . . . everything . . . Julie. I haven't broken it off with her yet, Emerson. I don't know how."

"It's a little early for that. Give me a number. How much?"

"More than $200,000."

"Now answer me honestly — did you take it?"

"Yes."

I wanted to punch him. I wanted to yell at him. I wanted a small loan.

"Where's the money? Did you spend it?"

"It's gone."

"But not spent."

"Gone. That's it."

"Where is it?" I asked again. He didn't answer. "If you did it, then why didn't you plead out when the grand jury brought the charges?"

Again he didn't answer. We were passing through east Dallas on an elevated highway, looking down on a collection of liquor stores and muffler shops. Matt said he needed gas, so we pulled off the highway to look for a twenty-four-hour gas station. We found one near White Rock Lake after looking for about twenty minutes.

"Matt, did you like me much?" I asked once we were back on the highway.

"We were friends . . . Still are."

"Yeah, but did you ever like me much? It's a little different."

He smiled. "Nope. But don't take it personally."

"I won't. It's sort of the same for me. I always knew how successful you'd be. You think like an accountant, a businessman.

You always have. I knew I'd never have money like you. I might have resented that a little."

"Your problem was you thought about everything too much. I hated it when you helped on my English papers. I didn't need an in-depth analysis of the social climate Dickens was trying to change. I needed a degree, and a C on that paper would have done just fine. I just wanted to make you feel good."

"So how'd we end up stuck with each other?" I asked with a grin of my own. "I wonder why we've been friends so long — and why I can't help but feel we're in it for life."

"Dunno. I don't mind much, though."

"Neither do I. I'm here to help you, Matt."

He didn't respond. I sat back and thought for a moment. If he'd stolen over $200,000, he sure was hiding it well, with the exception of the new-looking car. And for that matter, why would he need the money? His job as a CPA for North Texas Petroleum paid well — better than anything I'd ever see as a reporter. A drug problem? I watched his hands and his eyes. No telltale signs. It also didn't fit with the Matt I knew. Matt worked out, he listened to motivational tapes, he prayed frequently. Recreational drug use would be an unacceptable concept for him. But maybe if he was trying to get ahead at work, if he needed an extra boost around tax time . . .

No. Julie would have seen something, would have tried to get him some help.

"I can't figure it out, Matt," I said. "Why?"

"You wouldn't understand. You, of all people, wouldn't understand."

I was silent. The gulf between Matt and me was growing. "You're probably right. But was it worth it?" I asked. "If you plead guilty, you'll lose your job. You probably won't go to jail, but you'll have to pay back the money. That won't be easy. Who would hire a crooked accountant? Julie might stick by you, but would you want that for her? We both probably agree she deserves better than that."

"Yes, it was worth it . . . It will be worth it."

I studied Matt. He was tired. "Let's go home," I said. "Drop me at Danny's. I doubt that either of us is up for coffee."

He didn't say anything. Ten minutes later he pulled to a stop in front of Danny's door. My car was already in the parking lot.

"Don't bother with this, Emerson. Just let it happen. I can handle it. I'm a big boy. But thanks for being worried."

I nodded; that's exactly what I'd probably have to do. Matt drove off, and I walked to Danny's door. It was unlocked, so I let myself in. Danny was seated at his table, waiting for me.

"Anything?" he asked.

"Nothing. He told me he did it. He said it was worth it. He wants me to leave it alone."

"You can't do that. You know he didn't do it. He's got to be . . ."

"What? Lying? Covering for someone? Maybe, but who?"

Danny shook his head. "I'm going to bed," he said. "I've asked the pastor and the chairman of the deacons at Matt's church to meet with us tomorrow right after the service. You're working with the defense attorney, so it's okay — they said they would meet with us."

"Fine. But if nothing new emerges, I'm out."

"Okay. Good night."

That night I dreamed about Remington. It was personal stuff, it involved lip contact, and I'm not telling you anything more about it. The next morning Danny and I woke up, ate some breakfast, and went to church. We'd slept a little late, so we skipped Sunday school, but we were there for the main service at Hilltop Community Church, a few blocks from the college we'd all attended. The congregation was relatively small; about seventy-five people were at the service. The church had been built during our years in school; that's when Matt had joined.

It was a modern-looking metal building with perfunctory — not plush — carpet, and instead of real pews it had chairs that linked together. There were fake flowers on either side of the pulpit. Even the lighting was artificial.

The preaching was adequate but a little uninspiring. After a closing hymn Danny and I waited in our chairs. Eventually the preacher approached us and held out his hand. I took it. The preacher, a heavy-set man with jowls and a kind look to his light brown eyes, was wearing a suit that matched the building — functional, new-looking, but unimpressive with a hint of shabbiness.

"I'm Ed Aldridge," he said. "I'm the pastor here. Danny says you're working for Vernon Robbins. We'll talk to you, but there's not much we can tell you. We're only now starting to sort through the books and figure out what happened."

Another man came up behind him; this must be the chairman of the deacons. I shook his hand as well. He was a big man, tanned as if he'd spent most of his life out-of-doors. His hands were large and strong. The outsized, bulky knuckles were beginning to get arthritic; he'd been a fighter, I guessed. He minimized his shoulder movement, lifting only his forearm when he had reached for my hand.

"Emerson Dunn," I said.

"Willie Burson."

"Did you fight?"

Burson smiled. "Heavyweight. How'd you tell? I got my nose fixed years ago."

"The hands. Shoulders still sore from it?"

"A lot of years on the heavy bag, son."

"Let's meet in my office," Aldridge said. We followed him past the pulpit to a door by the choir loft. It led to a hallway, past some dressing rooms and some classrooms, and eventually to a glass-enclosed office. The same kind of carpet was in the office, and the chairs in front of the desk and stacked near a wall were the same kind we'd sat on during the service. Aldridge took his seat behind his desk and waited for us to assemble. I sat in a chair facing the desk, Danny sat beside me, and Burson sat on the edge of the desk, facing us. The office was relatively ornate, given the functionality of the rest of the church. It had Aldridge's diplomas and degrees on the wall, along with some framed prints. There were two enlarged photos on the wall to the left of the pastor's desk; both showed a smiling Aldridge with a woman I presumed was his wife, standing in front of historic ruins in Israel. In the background were other pastor-looking types. It looked as if Aldridge had signed up for one of those bulk-rate Holy Land tours. He noticed I was looking at the photos.

"It's a wonderful place," he said. "You should go sometime . . . Take a guided tour."

"I think I have a tour guide lined up," I said. "An Israeli friend who would never forgive me if I let anyone else show me around."

Aldridge smiled politely, as if he were pleased to hear I had a friend — any friend. "I suppose you have questions?" he asked me.

"Yeah. When did you first report this to the police?"

Aldridge looked at Burson. Burson raised his eyebrows a bit, then shrugged.

"We didn't," the former boxer said. "They came to us. Well, not the police, but federal investigators. Three months ago. We didn't know anything about it until then."

Aldridge picked up the slack. "They said they'd been doing a routine audit of our taxes, and in the expense report they came across some things that sent up some red flags."

"Like what?" I asked.

"A church our size sending out $200,000 in one year to a single foreign missions organization. Our entire yearly operating budget is barely $180,000."

"A missions organization? I thought it was supposed to be going to a missionary," I said, looking at Danny.

Aldridge picked up where'd he left off. "No . . . a group in Belize. I've only heard the group's name . . . The Belize Missions Foundation. I don't know anything about a particular missionary."

"Tell me the story from the beginning," I said after a moment. "Things aren't sounding kosher."

Burson looked at me with a puzzled expression and started talking. "I figure that all or most of the cash donations — not the checks — each week were put into a special account. Once a month Matt would wire the money to the group in Belize. Then it was wired somewhere else. We don't know where yet. Probably right back here to one of Matt's bank accounts. A quick thirty seconds' worth of effort, and he's got nice, clean money. Have you seen that new car he's driving?"

I began to feel a little defensive, probably much like Danny had felt when I questioned Matt's innocence. "I drive a '73 Ford, Mr. Burson. That doesn't mean I'm honest."

Burson paused. "You've made your point. Sorry. But now he's admitted it, hasn't he?"

I frowned. As far as I knew, the only people Matt had talked to about that were A. Vernon Robbins, Julie, and me. This was not a good rumor to be spreading.

"He told the court he's innocent," I said, and that was true. While Matt intended to tell the court otherwise, A. Vernon had thus far been successful in stalling him. So for the record, Matt was still pleading innocent.

"We don't know what to do," Aldridge said. "We asked about dropping the charges. The prosecutor said an indictment had already been handed down. Matt won't return my calls, so I can't minister to him."

"And to tell you the truth, the church has been hurt by this," Burson said. "Many in our congregation want to wash their hands of him, let him go to jail, and forget about him. We've had deacons' meetings every week since this began. This could cause wounds in our church body that I'm not sure would ever heal."

That was a bit melodramatic. I knew for sure that Matt was hurting, but it looked as if the church, as the aggrieved party, the victim, was going to turn him out. Another case of short-sighted Christians shooting their wounded. I looked over at Danny and flicked my eyes toward the door.

"I guess that's all we need," Danny said. "Thanks for your time."

We stood and shook hands with both men. Aldridge led us through the building and to the gravel parking lot outside. He stood at the door as we walked to Danny's truck and got in. We pulled away as Aldridge waved.

"Tell me about Burson," I said, "chairman of the deacons."

"I don't know him well," Danny said. "But I do know him. After graduation, when I was looking for a job, Matt introduced me to him. Mr. Burson has a construction business. Matt arranged it so I could work for him three days a week and look for a job in my field on the other days. He gets a lot of government work. We did a courthouse annex the summer I worked for him. I never saw Mr. Burson much. He'd come by the job site once or twice a day, but that was about it. He had engineers and foremen supervising the day-to-day work. After I found the job at First Baptist, Mr. Burson said I could always come back to work for him or use him as a reference."

"Sounds like a nice guy."

"He is."

"Now tell me about Aldridge."

"I only know him from when I visited the church with Matt. He's well-educated . . ."

Danny had his heart so set on going to seminary that I think he truly believed anyone who'd gone was well-educated. "Danny, who ran the meeting?"

"In there? What was there to run? You asked questions, and they answered."

"No, it wasn't that simple. Aldridge gave me some quick, easy answers, but Burson steered the conversation. When he started trying to focus on how Matt had hurt people instead of how or why Matt was hurting, I knew it was time to duck out. And another thing — Burson is the real power in that church. In a conflict, Aldridge would capitulate."

"What's that mean?"

"That means neither Aldridge nor Burson is where they should be spiritually. Not that any of us are, completely. But Aldridge is supposed to be the leader of that congregation, and Burson is supposed to submit to that leadership."

"You don't know that's not the case."

"You're right. I'm making an assumption based on a few minutes' worth of conversation. But that's part of my job — and that's a job I'm going to finish."

"You mean you'll help?"

"Yeah. Those two made me mad. They slandered someone I care about. There's mercy in this world, my friend, but I didn't see any of it in there. Not any at all."

6

When we got back to Danny's apartment, I reached for the telephone. I dialed the home number of an old friend, a guy who was now an assistant city editor for a Dallas newspaper. If I was going to do this, I was going to do it right. Doug Chen answered on the second ring.

"Hello?" He sounded a little annoyed. But then he always sounded annoyed when he answered the phone. Doug heard telephones ringing constantly at work, so when it happened at home, he took it as a personal affront.

"Afternoon, Doug," I said. "This is Emerson."

His tone changed perceptibly. "Dunn, how ya doin'?

"Fine. Listen, I'm in Dallas for a week or so, and I've got a story I want to pitch to you."

"Shoot. You were always one of my best stringers."

I'd worked for Doug a bit during my senior year of college. I covered a few suburban city council meetings for him as a free-lance reporter. If I was going to investigate Matt's case, I needed the backing of someone like Doug and the resources of the paper he worked for. I figured Doug would go for it, once I gave him a few vague details.

"It's about a church," I said. "The federal grand jury indicted the bookkeeper for embezzlement. I think it's a little more complicated than that."

"Churches always play well," he said. "Did we report the indictment?"

"No, and I was wondering about that. Don't you have someone at the federal courthouse every day checking those sorts of things?"

"Yeah. Feds must have wanted this one kept quiet. They tend to misplace the paperwork on those cases whenever my guy shows up. What's the peg?"

A "news-peg" is the event or angle you emphasize to make the story seem more timely. In the case of an indictment passed down a month ago, you needed something pretty solid, something to add a little newness to the news.

"One of two things," I said. "Either he's going to change his plea to guilty at the end of this week, or someone else is going to get busted. I don't know yet, but I have some weird feelings."

"I like your weird feelings. You always did come up with good stuff."

"I'll need your archives."

"You got it. But you aren't getting more than $250 for this piece, so watch your expenses. I have a budget, you know."

"You sound like a bureaucrat, Doug. But don't worry about the money. It's not the money I'm interested in. If I come up with anything you can print, you'll get your money's worth."

"I like you more and more as you get older, Dunn," he said. "When you gonna come work for me full-time?"

"Maybe someday, Doug. Maybe soon. We'll see. And thanks."

When I hung up, I noticed that Danny's face was having a few minor spasms. His eyes were getting kind of small, his cheeks were flushed, and he was having trouble keeping his mouth closed.

"Was it something I said?" I asked him.

"You'd use Matt for your career? You would print lies? In the Dallas newspaper?"

"This is the only way I know how to fight," I said. "I need to find out everything I can about Matt, the church, the pastor, this missions group. I need the paper's resources. If Matt does change his plea, well, the paper would run that anyway. If I can come up with more, then I'll be doing Matt a favor."

Danny was silent for a moment. "Can you come up with more?"

"I hope so, Danny. You were right all along. I know Matt, and I just can't believe he'd do something like this without some good reasons. We were on the right track last night. He's got to be covering for someone or hiding a bigger problem. He believes his career has ended, and he thinks he'll lose Julie. That's a lot for him to give up. That $200,000 wasn't worth his whole life."

"You should listen to me more," he said, finally smiling. "What can I do to help?"

"Nothing yet. I'm going to spend tomorrow in the newspaper's morgue."

Later that afternoon Danny got ready for work — he was running the sound at First Baptist's evening service — and I made another telephone call. About 275 miles away, Ricky answered the phone. Ricky was the son of Martin Paige, the pastor of the small Bible church I attended. Martin's family — his wife Meg and his three children — made a habit of feeding me and Remington after church on Sundays. I like that in a family. It was Martin who, ten years earlier at a small church outside Dallas, led me to Christ and then stuck with me for a few years while I figured out just what it was he'd gotten me into. Later we had found ourselves in the same small South Texas town together. He and his family had taken me in, and now they were taking in Remington and other various and sundry persons I brought "home."

Ricky, the middle child, was six years old and the only boy. I used that as a pretext to "be a big brother" to him, but the truth was that I simply enjoyed his company. I usually spent a good part of many Saturdays with him. On nice days we went sailing or played catch; on not-so-nice days we went to the library. This was the summer before Ricky's first grade year, but he already had a good handle on reading. We'd gotten through most of the Dr. Seuss books by the end of June. He sounded very literate when he answered the phone — greeting me, telling me who lived there and who was speaking, and asking if he could help me in any way. Meg must be working on telephone manners, I thought. I resisted the urge to make pig-noises into the phone — that would be juvenile and would hamper Meg's efforts, I decided.

"Hi, Ricky, this is Emerson."

"Hello. Where are you? Still in Dallas?"

"Yeah. You got any pretty girls over there who might want to talk to me?"

"I'll see." He paused. "We got some pretty girls, but they're eating. Remington said to tell you that she loves you, but her ice cream is melting on her cobbler."

"Dames. What do you do with 'em, Rick?"

We recited in unison, "Dames . . . You don't put your lips on 'em because you don't know where they've been!"

Okay, okay, maybe that was a little juvenile. I heard muffled objections in the background, and in a second Remington was on the phone.

"Gross! Did you teach him that?"

"Words to live by, dear. I've taught him that the same thing goes for frogs, turtles, and politicians. I'm helping shape his young mind. I think I'm doing a pretty good job of it."

"If that boy turns out twisted because of you . . ."

I heard Meg say something in the background about that being expected.

Remington just sighed into the phone in response to Meg's editorial comments. I bet Remington was wondering if all men were as charming as I.

"Do you miss me?" I asked.

"I'm not so sure now — but I guess so. Airborne does. He sulked all weekend. He was in my lap every time I sat down."

"That was just a ruse," I said. "He's playing on your sympathy. What are you doing letting an eighty-five-pound golden retriever sit in your lap, anyway?"

"When are you coming home?"

"I don't know yet. It's getting even more complicated. I agree with Danny now — Matt couldn't have just upped and stolen $200,000. There's more to it."

"Do what you can to help. Oh, Maggie's here, too. Want to say hi?"

Maggie was a new friend, one who had brought with her a bit of trouble, but she'd proven worth the effort. She was twenty-six and very pretty and had a past she didn't like to talk about much. But friends like Martin and Meg and Remington didn't make her talk about her past; they just concentrated on making her feel good about herself and finding real answers in the present. Maggie picked up another phone and said hello.

"I hear you're up in Dallas having a little vacation," she said. "If no one's shooting at you, it must be more relaxing than being down here."

"It's not so bad up here," I said. "I don't get cobbler and ice cream, though."

I remembered, at the mention of the dish and the notion of what all else Meg must have fixed, that Danny and I had forgotten about lunch.

"Well, don't worry about us," Maggie said. "I'll take Airborne to work with me tomorrow so he won't get lonely."

Maggie worked for David's uncle in a jewelry store he'd recently bought. David's Uncle Mordechai liked Airborne as much as he liked everyone else — in other words, completely and utterly. I knew he wouldn't mind having the dog at the shop, but there was no use in spoiling Airborne.

"You don't have to do that," I said. "He's got you girls fooled. He's a farm dog now. Leave him at the farmhouse."

"He's lonely," Remington said. "We'll take care of him. Besides, he's better behaved than you. He won't be any trouble."

I refrained from mentioning Mrs. Miller's chicken.

Maggie said good-bye and hung up her line.

"Is she staying at the house with you?" I asked Remington.

"Yes. I hope you don't mind. It gets scary at night . . . All those noises . . ."

"Yeah, that's the thing about nature. It's filled with animals and bugs and stuff. No, I don't mind. That just means there will be two of you tossing my place, looking for letters from old girl-friends."

"We already found them. Black briefcase in the back of your closet."

"I thought that was locked."

"If you want to keep something private, you should get a little variety in your life. You use the same four-digit code for everything — your ATM card, your briefcase, everything."

"Did you find anything incriminating?"

"Nothing much. Letters from Julie and some girl named Vicki. You can spill your guts about that one later. So tell me, how is Julie?"

"Fine."

"Is there anything you need to confess?"

"Nope," I said indignantly. "I've been good. Oh, we went to see Pete's band. He's doing fine. And Danny says hello."

Actually, Danny had only passed through the living room once, and he was looking for a missing shoe then, but I wanted to get off the subject of Julie.

"Tell them all hello for me," Remington said.

"I need to get ready for church, so I'll let you go. I love you."

"Me, too," she said. "I mean, I love you, too."

I heard Ricky snort/laugh in the way only six-year-old boys can. He saw my relationship with Remington as funny, but also awfully close to being a betrayal of my principles.

Remington hung up, and I looked at the phone for a moment. I wondered if I should ask her to come up in a few days. Danny came through and asked if I was ready to eat. He suggested we stop and get a burger on the way to church. I said that was fine. I was still wearing slacks and a button-down shirt and no tie, but I figured for First Baptist Church I ought to wear a tie. It was a pretty upscale congregation. I found one that was only mildly wrinkled in my suitcase and put it on. We left at about 4:30 for the 6 P.M. service. Danny had to be there half an hour early for the sound checks, so that gave us about an hour to find a burger. We went into someplace cheap and greasy, ordered, and sat down.

Danny looked thoughtful as he ate slowly. "Maybe he's not covering for anyone. Maybe he thinks it would just be over quicker if he pled guilty."

"Then why would he tell me he did it?"

"Yeah, I guess you're right. Still, I don't think he stole anything."

I didn't comment further. I just ate. About forty-five minutes later we drove up to the church. I found a seat toward the back and started reading a hymnal, waiting for the sanctuary to fill and the service to start. Danny was up above the balcony in the sound room. A guy who I assumed was scheduled to sing stood in front with a microphone, singing snatches of something I didn't recognize so Danny could check the level.

Before too long people started filtering in. A few greeted me, but for the most part everyone just said hello to their friends. I kept an eye out for A. Vernon Robbins; Danny had told me he'd be here tonight. About five minutes before 6:00 I saw him walk in with Mrs. Robbins, a woman who at one time could have become my mother-in-law. I got up and made my way to the couple. A. Vernon stuck out his hand. Mrs. Robbins (I never did learn to call her Carol) just smiled at me.

"I need the rest of the week, maybe more," I told the attorney as I shook his hand. "Can you hold Matt off that long?"

"I think so," he said. "What's your opinion?"

"I think you're right," I said. "He's willing to let this run right over him, but we shouldn't let it. So far I haven't found anything substantial; it's just a feeling. Somehow the whole situation just isn't kosher. Who's the U.S. attorney prosecuting this one?"

"Linda Chapman. If you want to meet with her, you'll probably have to go through me. Remember, she won't be able to talk about the case except to the defense attorney. I can arrange a meeting if you want."

"Not yet. Let me do some digging. By the way, do you know where the money went after it was wired to Belize?"

Vernon paused. "No, but Linda Chapman knows. That's supposed to come out in the discovery process, but so far she hasn't sent over any of the documents I've requested. She's stalling discovery."

"Does that mean she's not anxious to get this to trial?"

"It could mean that. It could also mean she doesn't have everything she wants us to think she has — bluff us into an easy confession. Less work on her part that way. Or she might not be paying much attention to this case. I'm sure she has dozens of others."

"I'm spending the day at the Dallas newspaper tomorrow," I said. "If anything interesting comes of this, I've promised it to them."

A. Vernon Robbins frowned a little. Lawyers, as a rule, don't trust newspapers much.

"That's the only way I could get into their archives," I explained. "And I need a little bit of weight behind me when I start asking questions."

A. Vernon nodded. His wife looked a little uneasy, as if questioning something. Then she spoke up. "This won't ruin Matt's reputation, will it?"

"It's ruined the moment he pleads guilty, ma'am," I said. "If we can keep him from doing that, and find out what's really going on, the damage will be minimized. I care about him as much as you do."

I thought for a moment. "Will he be here tonight?" I asked.

"No," Vernon said. "He's with Julie. He's not comfortable in church right now — any church. I can't say I blame him."

"I guess not," I said. We shook hands again, and the couple moved on. I sat down again, only to find that a couple with a very tiny baby had taken the seats next to mine. I smiled politely. The baby drooled and blathered in my general direction. And you wonder why I'm scared to death of the little guys.

The baby and I behaved decently throughout the service; he cried a little, but I didn't. After it was over, I waited for Danny by his truck. He found me about fifteen minutes after the service let out, and we drove home. We watched a little TV, then went to sleep without much fanfare or any deep conversation.

The next morning Danny was gone by the time I woke up. I had some dim memories of him bustling about earlier, but I'd pretty much slept through his whole morning routine. Good thing. He was annoyingly cheerful in the morning. Once in college, at about 5 A.M., he'd asked me what I had planned for such a fine morning. I tried to put him in the toaster.

7

I showered, got dressed in some jeans and a reasonably unwrinkled shirt, and headed downtown for the newspaper building. I found a parking lot that would only charge me about half of what my car was worth and crossed over a few blocks to the newspaper. I got a visitor's pass at the front desk and found my way to the archives — the newspaper morgue. While almost everything was on computer now, they still had shelves and shelves of articles clipped, dated, and filed by categories. I started my search.

Nothing on Matt. No one had taken note when he graduated, when he'd gone to work for one of the city's biggest firms, or when he'd gotten busted. Just a regular guy going about his regular business. Nothing newsworthy.

I checked on the church, Hilltop Community Church. Just one article, six years back when the building was finished and the congregation moved in. The article, clipped from the religion section, was about eight inches long; it had one paragraph on the pastor, Ed Aldridge. He became pastor of the congregation two years before the new building went up and had graduated from a seminary in Louisiana about ten years prior to that. It didn't say what he had done in the interim.

The building was built by Burson Contractors, Inc., the article said. Because Burson had given them the labor and materials at cost, the church didn't have to go into debt to pay for the building.

The article ended there. I sweet-talked a librarian into making me a copy of the article, although I doubted it would do me much good. I went back to my search.

I looked under "Belize Missions Foundation." Nothing.

Although I'd had no idea of what I was looking for, my morning wasn't turning out as productive as I had hoped. I decided to stick my head into Doug's office and let him know things weren't looking very spicy. I left the library and found my way to the newsroom; Doug's office was off to the side of it. The newsroom was high-tech but a jumble of controlled confusion nevertheless. I saw a few faces I recognized and nodded to them. I made my way through the desks and over to Doug's door. He was on the phone, but he waved me in.

His office was typical for a newspaper editor. It had framed copies of historic front pages on the walls, a smattering of awards, and irreverent notes to and from staff members. His desk was covered with copies of competing newspapers from throughout the area; although Dallas no longer had a second major metro newspaper, the smaller suburban papers were still capable of scooping the grand old rag on occasion.

I sat down in a remarkably clean chair and faced Doug. He was telling someone that he didn't want to hear about their problems and that if they wanted someone to confess to, call the cops or Rome. Doug was a sensitive guy, but he hid it well. He hung up and gave me an expectant look. He was short and thick and hairy, and I'm afraid that made him resemble an impatient groundhog. But he still sounded like a newsman: sarcastic.

"Already?" he said wonderingly. "You're done with the story exposing the scandal of the century already?"

"Not even close," I said. "I'll have something for you, but I don't know what. It's not panning out like I had hoped."

"Well, what *do* you have?"

"I've got a guy accused of stealing $200,000 from a small church over a one-year period. The way the math works out, that's more than the church's entire annual operating budget. So the Feds nail him. But I know the guy; he isn't greedy, he isn't sloppy, and what's more, he shows no sign of any extra wealth."

"That's pretty serious . . . stealing from a church. And that's a lot of money. Why did it take them a whole year to figure it out?"

"What do you mean?"

"It's a small church, right?"

"Yeah."

"So if that big a chunk of your income was suddenly missing, and none of the big givers had left, wouldn't you notice?"

I thought about it. He was right. Even if Matt had unchecked access to the books, someone would have noticed a drop like that. What had Burson said about just the cash donations? More than $200,000 was donated in cash? That didn't add up either. It would mean $4,000 cash in the offering plate each Sunday — from a grand total of seventy-five or so regularly attending members.

"Who's in charge there?" Doug asked.

"The pastor is a guy named Aldridge . . . Passive guy . . . The real power appears to be a guy named Burson."

"Burson?"

"Willie Burson, a contractor . . . Chairman of the board of deacons."

Doug frowned, then reached over to his telephone. He dialed four numbers and hit the Speaker button. I heard a male voice answer, "Yes?"

"Warrick? Can you come in here for a moment?"

Doug turned back to me. "Wayne Warrick is one of my county government reporters. He might have a line on Burson. Burson runs a very active contracting business here. He's done almost every Dallas County project for years now. He has a knack for being the low bidder."

A guy a little older than me entered. Warrick was blond and balding. He took a seat next to me and looked at his boss.

"Tell Mr. Dunn what you know about Burson Contractors, Inc."

"It's a scam," Warrick said, turning to me. "Burson is getting too many lucrative government contracts. A county building here, a sheriff's substation there. He must have a man inside the county purchasing agent's department — that's the department that sends out for bids. He's got to be greasing a few palms to get as many contracts as he has."

"What can you get out of the purchasing agent's department?" I asked.

"Nothing. We've tried. It must be one person, one very secretive person. So far, though, we're the only ones who have noticed anything strange. The county auditor seems to think everything's okay, and the district attorney isn't interested. We asked for an investigation, and they looked into it for about two hours. On every project he was awarded, Burson was the low bidder. So, no investigation. They think he just works cheap."

"How about going in the back door? Have you tried to get to someone inside Burson's company?"

Doug answered that one. "Warrick has asked to do that. He had it all figured out. He'd go on as day labor and keep his eyes open, talk to the foreman and hopefully to Burson. But I can't spare the manpower on that sort of thing without more evidence of some wrongdoing."

"Let's say I've got a man. How would I do it?"

"I've got the address of all the job sites," Warrick said. "You go to each one and ask for a job. If they need someone they'll hire you on the spot — for the day or week or whatever."

"Dunn, won't Burson recognize you?"

"Yes, he would. I have someone else I could send in . . . a foreign guy who's pretty strong. He'll look more like a construction worker than I do."

"I can pay a little more for this — probably $200 to each of you."

"I'm sure that would be fine with him. If you let me use your phone, I'll give him a call."

Doug handed me his phone, and I dialed David's beeper number. When the tone sounded, I punched in the number of Doug's line, then hung up.

"Get Dunn the list of addresses," Doug said to Warrick. Warrick left the room and returned just as the telephone rang. I answered it.

"David, this is Emerson," I said.

"You need me? I'll tell Sherri. She can run the film. I'll be there in five hours."

No questions, no comments, no hesitation. He was ready to come up to Dallas.

"No need to rush," I said. "Remember how to get to Danny's apartment?"

He said he wasn't sure; I gave him some quick directions. He told me he'd be there by 8 P.M.

"Thanks, David," I said. "And bring your camera and some work clothes."

"Okay."

We hung up, and I looked at Doug. "He's a good man," I said. "But it's going to take more than just a few passing comments from a foreman to nail Burson if he's really getting government contracts improperly."

Doug grinned. "You know me, Emerson. I never let the lack of hard facts stop me from publishing a story. If comments from the foreman are all we get, we'll confront Burson with the comments. He'll deny it, and we'll run a story about him saying he doesn't get the contracts improperly. Even if that's all we have, it will be enough the kick the D.A. into gear with an investigation. And once again we'll be the white knights riding to the rescue of the taxpayer."

"What if he's innocent?"

"Then he'll sue our pants off, and we'll print a retraction; he'll come out looking like an honest businessman beaten up by the biased and vicious media. That kind of thing could get him elected to a council seat or even mayor. And we'll all go on about our business."

I smiled. "Great. The guy I'm sending in is a photographer. What kind of art would help?"

"If you get me a shot of Burson or anyone but Burson's engineer meeting with anyone from the county purchasing agent's department, we'll run it on the front page and then frame it."

"Why not Burson's engineer?"

"He could say the engineer was just going over bid specifications. No one else will have that excuse."

"I see. We'll get what we can on this."

"Great," Doug said. "You don't have a deadline, but check in with me every other day or so."

I said I would, and I thanked Wayne Warrick for the list of job sites. I left the newspaper building and found my car. I paid the overinflated parking fee and pointed the car east, toward my parents' house. I'd been in town for three days now, and I hadn't been by to see them. My mother was going to let me hear about that. I found my way through east Dallas to Mesquite, a suburb just south of Garland. My parents lived in a subdivision in north Mesquite, near the shopping centers and restaurants that had been a cow field a few years ago when I was in high school.

I took the I-635 South exit off Interstate 30, then the Town East Boulevard exit off I-635. I drove east a few more miles, found my parents' street, and pulled into their driveway a few minutes later. My mother's car was blocked in the narrow driveway by my father's VW van; they were both home. I figured they would be. My father taught music at the local high school, and my mother taught English at the local junior college. Hence my first name: Emerson. Who else but an English teacher would saddle a kid with that? My mother even looked like an English teacher — slightly unkempt, graying hair, little makeup, but a warm smile.

I parked in the street up against the curb in front of their house. It was a cookie-cutter house, red brick that looked exactly like every third house on the block. Some shutters that were never meant to shut were painted a slate blue, as were the few pieces of wood trim around the house. The lawn looked good; my father expended a lot of effort on that lawn. I think it was because it got him out of the house.

My mother had seen my car; she was waiting at the door for me. After a hug, her first question was whether I had eaten. I assured her I hadn't, but that eating wasn't my sole purpose in visiting. She sounded relieved and said in a low voice that my father was in the garage, destroying the plumbing in and around the washing machine. I had inherited his utter lack of mechanical ability, but I said I'd go out and help.

I went through the kitchen to the door to the garage. I opened the door and found my father indeed doing his best to kill the plumbing.

"It leaks," he said, motioning at one of the hoses running to the washer.

"Did you fix it?"

He nodded. "Now it leaks more."

I nodded. Things usually went that way when my father took up a tool. I looked at the old guy. He was pushing sixty, and I had no questions about what I'd look like at that age. He was a little heavier than me — maybe twenty pounds — but neither of us would ever be truly fat. Other than a few wrinkles here and there, we looked exactly alike. At least Remington knew what she would be getting herself into.

"Where's the leak?" I asked.

"By the wall." Again he pointed with the wrench.

"What did you do to fix it?"

"I tightened it. I think I stripped it."

I looked closely. The hose was connected to the faucet in a crooked sort of way and was still dripping onto the garage floor.

"Yup. I think we can fix it." I turned off the faucet, then took the wrench and loosened the hose to the washer. Luckily the little brass shavings left on the faucet showed that the brass threads on the hose had been stripped, not the steel threads on the faucet. I detached the end of the hose connected to the washing machine. "Let's go get one of these," I said.

We took my dad's VW van to a local hardware store and found the replacement. Let me stress that this sort of father-and-son fix-it thing was not common. He was not the sort of father who took me out to the garage and taught me how to use power tools. He didn't own any power tools. For a few years we did our best with baseball — but we both lacked any talent for the game whatsoever, despite our mutual love for it. We finally gave up when we took out a window in my mother's car with a wild pitch. He took the blame for that one.

My father didn't teach me about sports and tools; instead, he taught me about some of the most beautiful things in the world: a 12-bar blues progression; a Bach mass; anything and everything Beethoven produced that involved a piano. I heard Cole Porter tunes in my crib and the Boston Symphony throughout my childhood.

As with baseball, the love didn't translate into talent. While my father had studied at Juliard, I was the sort of student who frightened music teachers. Instead, I found I was more adept at writing; my mother helped there. The poor woman could barely keep me in books, and I spent entire summers at the library. Watergate hit at a formative time in my life — as it did with an entire generation of current journalists — and my heart was set. I read everything on journalism I could find; my mother tried to temper that with Literature now and then.

My parents did their best with what they had to work with, I guess. They were mystified when I started going astray in high school. My grades dropped, my attendance record was embarrassing, and I was often seen with The Wrong Crowd. My father was teaching at a different high school, but he had his sources. They found out I was having some problems with drugs, but I wasn't ready to accept any help. I finally dropped out of school early in my senior year when it became clear I wouldn't pass without a significant amount of effort, more effort than I was willing to put forth. After that smart move, it wasn't more than a year before I was burned out on amphetamines and minimum-wage jobs and ready for help.

My parents gave me what they could — a room to come home to, regular meals. My dad even made a few calls and helped me get a job at a newspaper, something I'd about given up on. It was at the newspaper that I met Martin Paige, a pastor, and he took it from there. He showed me that Christianity was a pretty great thing; he showed me where to find the hope I'd lost during a rough adolescence. My parents were amazed at the change; I think for the first time in years, they were learning to be proud of me again.

My relationship with my father had suffered the most during the rough years; it was now on a solid foundation and getting better all the time. He wasn't a man who spent a great deal of energy talking. Remington once remarked that although she'd spent several weekends in his company, she'd never heard him say more than three sentences at a time. But that was something I was always comfortable with. In his van on the way home from the hardware store we didn't speak at all. But it was a healthy silence; it was our way of telling each other we were comfortable.

When we arrived back at my parents' house, my mother had

thawed out some pork chops, getting them ready for my father to grill. It took about ten minutes to attach the hose; we turned on the water, and the hose didn't leak. Success.

We sat in the kitchen and talked for about an hour, with my dad going outside every few minutes to check the grill. Mom made some veggies to go with dinner and did a good job of not burning anything. They asked pointed questions about Remington, and then we talked about Matt's problems. They remembered Matt from college; they didn't think he would steal close to a quarter-mil either.

As we ate, my dad asked about Airborne. I said Airborne was fine and was currently being spoiled rotten by pretty women. My dad said that was typical. He said I ought to ask for pointers. I said I thought it had something to do with being furry and fluffy, but that I had inherited a receding hairline. He nodded.

After dinner I said I had to go; I wanted to drop in on Matt and get a little more information. I promised I'd try to stop by again before I left for home, and I said I'd be sure to bring David along.

I called Matt from my parents' kitchen; no answer. I called Julie's apartment, and she said he was there.

"Can I come by for a few minutes? I have some things to discuss with Matt."

She hesitated. "Sure . . . Come on over."

"I'll be there in half an hour."

I then dialed Danny's number. Danny was there, but David hadn't shown up yet. I said I'd be back by 7:00 or so.

It actually took me less than twenty minutes to drive up I-635 to north Dallas and Julie's apartment. Julie answered the door wearing a business suit; Matt was uncharacteristically wearing jeans. Either that was a hefty six o'clock shadow or he hadn't shaved that morning. He obviously hadn't gone to work that day. Not that I was against that. He was wearing a faded polo shirt that was wrinkled enough to have been in a real polo match, albeit as a saddle blanket. In short, Matt didn't look good. That was rare for him.

Julie invited me into her living room. Matt was watching the news on her television and sitting on the undefinable sofa. I sat across from him on one of the similarly undefinable chairs and studied his face. Nope. No $200,000 in extra income; if he had that kind of money, he would have shaved.

"Matt, tell me what you know about Willie Burson."

Matt turned his attention from the television to me. His eyes started to show comprehension that I wasn't backing off from his problem, and with that comprehension came anger. "What do you want to know about him for?"

"For the Dallas County D.A., for starters," I said. "Is he clean?"

"He's got nothing to do with me. Leave him out of this."

"That's not what I think. Did you tell him you want to plead guilty?"

Matt looked even more annoyed. "I haven't talked to him. Neither should you."

There was almost a note of concern in his last sentence. "Is that because he's stealing government contracts?" I asked. "You know me. I love corruption. It's sort of my specialty. Tell me how corrupt he is, Matt."

Matt looked back at the television. "He's a deacon in my church," he said without looking at me. "I don't know anything else about him."

"Then tell me about Aldridge."

Matt's eyes snapped back to meet mine. "Looking for dirt on him, too? Leave him alone. He's a good man. I owe him a lot. He's been like a father to me."

Matt's glance strayed to Julie, who was off to my right. "No one's perfect, Emerson," he said.

"No one has asked you to be, Matt. I just want you to be open with me."

Matt shook his head. "I can't. You wouldn't understand. You only know corruption. That's your specialty, remember?"

I guess I'd gotten myself into that one. I gave up. Matt wasn't cooperating. "Never mind then," I said, standing. "You act as if you want your life to go down the tubes. A lot of people care about you, Matt."

He didn't respond. Julie, who was looking on from the doorway to the kitchen, shrugged, as if to say she didn't know what was wrong with him either.

I made for the door; Julie followed. I paused at the door for a moment, and Julie hugged me. "Don't let him do this to himself," she whispered.

"I've got the cavalry coming up," I said in a similarly low voice. "You've never met David, but you will soon. I still think we've got a shot at saving this jerk. Tell him to shave."

Julie smiled. I turned and walked out the door without looking back. It was a few seconds before I heard the door shut. Where had that kind of loyalty been when she was engaged to me, I wondered. I put the thought out of my mind as I started my car and headed to Danny's. I had an Israeli to brief.

As I drove, I wondered about David's willingness — no, change that to his *urgency* — to come up and help me. He knew none of the details, but even if he did, he'd have still taken off work and driven up. Perhaps I had supplanted his thoughts about Gershom. Our relationship had changed recently. Before, I sort of took care of him. I took David places, helped him with his English, and hopefully soothed some of the loneliness he must have felt as a new immigrant.

But lately, especially after recent events in which he'd done a pretty decent job of getting me out of trouble with guys who saw violence as a form of family recreation, he was starting to feel as if *he* were taking care of *me*. Not that I minded. A trained Israeli soldier is a pretty potent friend to have on your side. His news instincts were good, too.

When I arrived at Danny's apartment, David's Toyota was in the parking lot. I looked at my watch; it was 6:45. I went in and found David and Danny talking politics. An Israeli will usually take any opportunity to talk politics, David once told me. That and criticizing the small nation's tax structure were the national pastimes, he said.

"Hello, David," I said as I flopped down in Danny's overaged recliner.

"What's up, Emerson?"

"Well, it's a long story." I told it as concisely as I could, without omitting the important stuff.

"You want me to be a construction worker?"

"Yeah," I said, "if you don't mind too much."

"No problem. I can put brick down."

"Lay brick." His English wasn't perfect yet. We were working on it.

"Yeah, lay brick," he said. "And some carpentry. What am I looking for?"

"Anything that might show Burson is getting the government contracts illegally. See if anyone high-up brags about having a friend in the county courthouse. We'll do it this way for the rest of the week and see what we come up with. This might be completely unrelated to Matt's problems, but I doubt it."

David smiled. "Will I get shot at this time?"

"I don't think so," I grinned. "Will you miss it?"

"A little. You and Ruth keep my life from being boring, that's for sure."

We resumed the discussion of politics. We concluded we were against them. The perfect form of government, we decided, would have us three as the heads of state. We would pledge that once put into power we would immediately leave for a small Caribbean island where we wouldn't bother anyone. I said that perhaps I should be elected Chief King Over The Two Other Guys, but for some reason Danny and David disagreed.

David had brought an inflatable mattress and a sleeping bag with him; he said he'd be fine on the floor. Before we went to sleep I gave him the list of addresses of job sites, and Danny came up with a map of Dallas. We found a site near the college, on the west side of town. Burson was building a sheriff's department substation. We figured David could apply to work as day labor; he had a pretty good shot, according to Danny, who'd done it himself. David looked strong, he had experience, and he was willing to work cheap. Danny said that Burson didn't skimp on labor, because it would all be paid for by the county. And later, if things were going well, David could strike up a casual conversation with the foreman about what other jobs the firm was engaged in. It was the start of a plan, at least. I knew David could wing it from there.

The next morning he was up before dawn. He left after a quick bowl of cereal, heading for the site near Mountain Creek Lake. He worn old jeans and a blue work shirt, along with some steel-toed boots he'd brought. He carried Danny's lunch pail and a Thermos and looked pretty authentic. He planned to mention Danny as the person who'd told him there might be work there. That couldn't hurt.

Danny left for work about an hour later.

Now it was my turn. After a quick shower, I decided it was time to do a little infiltrating of my own. But first I had to do some information gathering. I looked up Burson Contractors, Inc. in the phone book and dialed the number. The listing also had an address — Coit Road, an area I knew. Good. A woman answered the telephone a second later.

"Burson International," she said.

"Is this Burson Contractors?" I asked, a little confused.

"Yes, it is. We're now Burson International."

"If I had a billing problem, whom would I speak to?"

"Accounts payable, sir. I'll connect you," she said.

"No, no, not payable — receivable. I don't think I received

the right bill. It's not anywhere near what I think I owe you."
Actually, I hadn't received a bill at all. In technical journalism
terms this was called "lying." I'd have to talk to Martin about
the theological implications later.

"Looks like a big mistake," I said. "Could cost you guys some
money if we don't get it worked out. Who's your top bean-
counter?"

"That would be Dick Freid. He's unavailable at the moment.
Can I take your number?"

"No, I'll just drop the bill in the mail with a note, showing
what I think I owe you. I'll be happy to send a check as soon as
we figure out exactly how much I do owe."

"That will be fine, sir," she said and hung up.

I had a name. When you have a name, it's only a matter of a
little legwork to find a face, and then you have someone to
bother. I looked in Danny's desk drawers until I found some
paper and envelopes. I sat down and wrote out a letter to Mr.
Freid.

Dick, it read. *I know about the jobs. So do others. But I can help
you. Meet me at the flower shop in the Preston Village Shopping
Center at 5 P.M. Urgent.*

I put the letter into an envelope and sealed it. I put Freid's
name and Burson International's address on it. I grabbed a
bagel from Danny's kitchen (we'd have to help restock the place
before we left) and headed out the door. I drove downtown to
the office of a courier company. For a mere $15 my little letter
would be hand-delivered to Freid by noon. I paid a man whose
business attire as a courier was fancier than anything I wore to
work. I figured I'd go over to the courthouse to do a little more
digging.

The Dallas County Courthouse is a maze of small, over-
crowded offices. It took me about forty-five minutes to find my
way to the purchasing department. A gray-haired woman at a
desk near the door asked if she could help me, and I said I was

looking for the animal control department. She patiently explained it was in another building, then kindly gave me directions to that building. The whole time I was trying to memorize the faces of the bureaucrat-types who were wandering to and fro. I counted the number of desks in the front room and the number of individual offices. I think the lady was getting annoyed at my inattentiveness to her directions, because she was abrupt when she asked if there was anything else I needed.

"No thanks, Toots," I said. Every abrupt little old lady needs to be called "Toots" now and then.

I left the office and then stood around the elevators down the hall for a while. When an elevator going up would stop, I'd say I was waiting for one going down. When one would stop on its way down, I'd say I was waiting to go up. Within two hours, almost everyone from the purchasing department had gone up or down or past me down the hall.

I had a decent fix on the faces, I thought. Seven I knew I would recognize if I saw them again. About a dozen others had gone in or out of that office, and I figured I had a moderate to good chance of identifying them if I saw them with a Burson person.

You learn a lot about the county government waiting by the elevators, I discovered. By the time I was ready to leave, I knew better than to date Yvonne because of the way she treated Glenn and then Mike in the auditor's office; I knew about Shannon's new baby, although I never found out if Shannon was the mother or the father. The county judge was either a complete idiot or the only man in the courthouse with a brain, depending on to whom you listened. And I learned the many reasons why I should never eat at the courthouse cafeteria.

My watch said it was my lunchtime, and since the cafeteria was something I was now afraid to risk, I left the courthouse and went to my car. I drove north from downtown until I reached Preston Road. I found a burger joint and wasted some time. At about 3 P.M. I went over to the flower shop in the Preston Village Shopping Center. I paid $30 for a little arrangement of flowers, to be delivered to Dick Freid at Burson International. I kept the receipt. Maybe Doug would reimburse me. I filled out a little card to go with the arrangement. It said, "It was good to see you, Dickie. Love, Me." The florist assured me it would be delivered first thing in the morning. I told the florist to leave a few business cards with Dickie, too, because he might want to use him in the future. The florist smiled and said he would do that. I took note of the faces in the shop, then went back to my car, which was parked about four rows from the florist's front door. I rolled down my windows and waited.

Waiting in an unmoving car in Dallas in July is not a comfortable occupation. But I figured it was better than working at a construction site in Dallas in July, so I didn't complain.

If Freid was smart, he'd ignore my letter to him. If he was nervous, he'd show up at 5 P.M. just like it said. If he was really nervous, he'd show up early and wait outside to see who went in to meet him. Then he'd know whether to go in or not.

I was guessing nervous; I was wrong. Freid was really nervous. He showed at 4:10 and parked three rows in, right in front of the flower shop. He sat in his blue BMW with the motor running for a while. Not very subtle, but then he was an accountant, not an investigative reporter. Dickie was a fat man who was sweating even before he turned his air conditioner and engine off at 4:28. He was balding and graying, and he had a mustache. He wore a tie. That's about all I could see from my car. I stayed low, behind the big steering wheel of my Ford. Still, it never occurred to him to watch for someone watching him. If he'd been looking for me, he'd have spotted me. Instead, his eyes were glued to the front door of the florist's shop and to the cars pulling up to it. He got fidgety as it drew closer to 5:00. At ten minutes after, he pulled out quickly. I think the pressure must have gotten to him. I pulled out slowly and followed him down Preston Road. We wove through north Dallas traffic for a while. We went into a residential area off Hillcrest just north of the loop, and I watched Freid pull into an unassuming one-story brick house. I noted the address. Then I drove toward Danny's, knowing I could find Freid at Burson's in the morning.

I arrived at Danny's apartment before either of the other guys. The phone rang, and it was a female voice asking for Danny. I assumed this must be the new girlfriend, so I introduced myself. She said her name was Paula and that Danny had mentioned me. She also said they had a date that night and asked if I wanted to come since I was visiting. She probably just didn't want to be rude. I was probably supposed to decline, but I didn't. That'll teach her. I asked if I could bring a well-behaved friend if I made him shower first, and she said I could.

When Danny came in, I told him about our date.

"And she invited you guys?" he said.

"Yeah. What a nice gal. I hope you don't mind."

"Me? No, I don't mind. I'm trying to build a relationship based on honesty and trust and caring and sensitivity. If you guys come along, I can show her what the alternative to those qualities are. You're actually doing me a favor."

I couldn't find anything to throw at him, so I ate some more of his food. I had cleaned out an entire giant box of animal crackers in the four days I'd been there, I realized, in addition to everything else we'd eaten. It was a start.

David came in a little after 6:00. He looked tired but happy.

"How did it go?" I asked.

"Good. I went to the trailer at the job and asked for the fore-man. He asked what did I want, I told him I want to work. I said Danny Stockman had sent me; he said he remembered Danny. He said he'd try me for a day, but only to clean up where the other men were working. I said that's fine. I worked hard, and after lunch the foreman asked if I knew anything about pouring concrete. I did, so I helped pour a slab. He said I can come back tomorrow. I'll ask about other Burson jobs then."

I told the guys about my day, and they were a little curious as to why I would want to arbitrarily bother someone.

"Because sooner or later he's going to get nervous enough to make a mistake," I said. "If I'm lucky he's going to meet with someone from the courthouse soon to see if they know what's going on. If anyone knows about the contracts, it would be Freid."

"That sounds good," Danny said. "I hope it works."

"So do I."

We all took showers to get ready for our date. Danny was taking Paula out to dinner, so we wanted to look our nicest. David even shaved again. Danny had several sorts of aftershave on the shelf in his bathroom, and since David and I couldn't decide which one to use, we played mix-and-match. Paula was going to meet us at the apartment, and we'd leave from there.

"In two cars," Danny said.

We nodded. "Can she ride with us?" David asked.

"No."

Paula arrived at about 7:30. She was pretty, with long hair and a nice smile. Danny was doing okay for himself. We ate at the Old Spaghetti Warehouse in Dallas's West End. David still ate as if he were in the army — fast, with a minimum of table manners and decorum but a maximum amount of efficiency. He cleaned his plate quickly. In the army, especially in combat, he had never known when he was going to get called out or when he'd eat next. Paula didn't seem offended, and she asked a lot about his home. She sounded fascinated. She asked Danny about work. He was working with another sound engineer to put a series of sermons by First Baptist's pastor on tape; so for a while, in addition to the Sundays and the frequent weeknight work, Danny would be going to the church from 9 to 5 every day.

It turned out that Paula worked at the church as well. She was a teacher in the school run by the church; she had a class of second-graders.

"That's a nice age," I said, thinking of Ricky.

"It's my favorite," she said. "They're young enough to still want to please you. By the time they get to fifth and sixth grades, they're ready to rebel a little, to test their boundaries."

"By the time they're in junior high, they're ready to test your sanity," I said. "I teach a junior high Sunday school class."

"His fiancée helps," Danny added. I kicked him under the table.

"Are you getting married, Emerson?" Paula asked with a touch of surprise. I don't know if it was surprise that Danny hadn't told her or surprise that someone would marry me. I gave her the benefit of the doubt since she seemed like a nice lady.

"Well . . ." I started, trying to think of a nice way to say, "Not unless I can overcome this phobia I have of tuxedos and binding vows." But before I could say anything David spoke up.

"He might not know it yet, but he is," David said. I kicked him, too. He ignored it. "In fact, I think he's the only one who doesn't know. And I tell you, my friend," he said, turning to me, "if you don't get on with it, you're going to lose Remington. I would not like to see that happen."

He smiled and put his arm around me. Israelis are very demonstrative. "Emerson would be lost without this woman," he said. "The sooner he realizes this, the better."

I considered elbowing him, but we were supposed to behave for the nice lady.

"Is that true, Emerson?" the nice lady said.

"It's a little premature," I said. "We haven't even discussed marriage . . . much."

"So you have talked about it?" Danny said.

"A little. Dumb things . . . Like when I brought my dog down,

I checked to see if she would mind if we kept him inside. And we've talked about what I would call her if her last name changed. I think we settled on Cathy. I'd probably call her Remington, anyway."

"You're just a romantic fool, aren't you?" Danny said.

"That's me. So, Dan the Man, how long have you two been dating?"

Paula perked up at this; Danny looked a little uncomfortable. He deserved it.

"Seven weeks now, right?" she asked him. "We met at church."

The rest of the evening passed fairly quickly. In the interests of politeness, Paula asked David a lot about himself in addition to the questions about Israel, but David managed to give a lot of one-word answers. He did talk about Ruth some though. We finished up a little before 9:45. Danny said he was going to stop with Paula somewhere and get some coffee. If I didn't know him better, I'd have thought he was just trying to ditch us so he could be alone with a girl. Luckily I knew him better.

Once in the car, David started talking a little more. We talked about the set-up at his new "job," and we even discussed possible new ways to annoy Freid. Then he got quiet for a few moments.

"Thinking about Gershom?" I asked.

"The whole war, really. It wasn't so many years ago."

"It was 1982, right?"

"Early June. My tank corps crossed the border on June 6."

"D-Day," I said.

"What?"

"That's the day the Allies invaded France, remember?"

"Oh, yeah. This was like that at first. We had a clear purpose; we also had a new government. The Likud Party had gotten in, after the Labor Party had run things for so long. At first everything was 'Peace for Galilee.' We would drive out the PLO and then go home. Lebanon was at war with itself; you had the Shi'ites, the Maronites, the Syrians, the Druze. What was one more faction? We reached Beirut in a week. Everyone was behind us. But that didn't last long. We got bogged down; we became occupiers. Then the second-guessing began. The Labor leaders said they were against it. I was a soldier; I knew we had done some good. I was attached to the Golani Brigade. We were the first in. We took Beaufort Castle, a PLO base on a mountain in southern Lebanon. We eventually drove Yasir Arafat from Beirut. That was in August. But then, in September, came Sabra and Shatila."

"What are those?"

"Were. They were refugee camps. Our allies in Lebanon, the Phalangists, went into a camp being guarded by us, the Israelis, and killed everyone. They were supposed to be mopping up terrorists still hiding in the camps, but they killed civilians. Almost a thousand. The Israeli soldiers knew, or at least had a good idea about, what was going on in the camps. They could hear the screams, but . . . they didn't respond. I wasn't there. I was across the city. I didn't know about it for two days. It made me sick, but what could I do? So the invasion was, I suppose, our Vietnam. I was there for more than a year."

"Do you think it was wrong?"

"No. Perhaps the methods were wrong, and our goals weren't very clear, but our motives were right, I think. Still, it wasn't a hero's war. My father died in the 1967 war — the Six Day War. That was a hero's war. Gershom died, but not as a hero."

I nodded. There wasn't much I could say. David was silent, too. We drove to Danny's apartment and parked. We went in and didn't talk much more before we went to sleep. I offered David the couch, since he was doing real work while I was just having a little fun with a bean-counter, but he declined. He said something about not going soft.

In the morning we were all up by 5:30 — why, I don't know. Personally I consider 8 A.M. a painful hour, but David had to get ready for another day of real, live, sweaty work. Danny was preparing to leave early for his job, too. I was getting ready for another hot day in Dallas.

David didn't mention anything more about Gershom, but then he wasn't the type to dwell on the past. Instead, he seemed in a good mood and even made breakfast.

"I'll talk to the foreman today," he said. "I think he likes me.

I work fast, and I don't complain. And I'm cheap. I'll ask him what other jobs the company has, for when this one is finished. Maybe he will talk about the county business."

David and I left the apartment at about the same time, after trying to get Danny to divulge some details about his late-night coffee tryst with Paula. He didn't, so we pledged not to tell him anything about our love lives. He said he didn't care about our love lives. He had a good point, so we left. David went to his construction site, and I went to stake out Burson International.

It was just after 7 A.M. when I parked across the street from Burson's office on Coit Road. It was a small, one-story, six-office complex, with Burson International sort of in the middle. The building was in the center of a busy block, but I could still see across Coit, through the traffic. I was parked in a pizza joint's lot, facing the road. I had three newspapers, a leftover bagel from breakfast, and a Thermos full of cold orange juice. I figured I'd get lunch at the pizza joint.

Freid arrived in his BMW at 8 A.M. sharp. Punctual. I liked that. I only caught a glimpse of him as he parked and marched into the office, but I could see he wasn't a happy man. At about 9 A.M., the florist's delivery person arrived with my flowers. The delivery person — an older man, probably a bored retiree with a part-time job — went in with a smile but came out scowling. I could understand. Florist delivery people have great jobs as a rule: they drive around all day making people happy. It must have come as a surprise to him that Freid was less than pleased to receive the flowers. But that was my goal: knocking Freid off balance.

About two minutes after the delivery man left, a woman came out the Burson front door and walked slowly to her car; she was looking around the whole time. She slowly took her purse from over her shoulder, slowly found her keys, and slowly opened her trunk. She held it open for a few moments and then closed it, without ever looking in it. Instead she was studying the cars in surrounding parking lots and the windows in surrounding stores and offices. When she closed her trunk she slowly turned toward the street, where she probably couldn't see me through the traffic and through the windshield, especially if I ducked down a little.

So I didn't duck down a little. I waved. I figured subtlety had gone out the window with the flowers, so I grinned and waved even harder. If she'd been closer I would have winked. She ignored me, but I could tell she had seen me. Next time I'd send flowers to *her*. I bet her name was Babs. She looked like a Babs. She went back inside quickly. It was the first thing I'd seen her do quickly.

Surveillance isn't all it's cracked up to be. For the most part, it's boring. It would have been boring that day except for a few minor incidents. The first incident — after Babs, I mean — came at about 9:15. A navy-blue Cadillac drove into the Burson parking lot. It had a car phone antenna, vanity plates that read "Burson," and Willie Burson himself in the driver's seat. This time I ducked down. He ignored me, but I could tell he noted my car when he glanced across the busy street. He walked inside and stayed inside for about five minutes. Then he came out and left.

That meant Freid had gotten scared enough to call his boss. Now it all depended on how much he told his boss. If Freid was a strict self-preservationist, he might have told Burson just that someone was following him and had sent him flowers. He might have left out the part about my note.

Or he might have spilled everything, in which case Burson would probably have time to cover his tracks, whatever those tracks might be.

This wasn't the way I had hoped it would go. I'd hoped Freid would talk to his county government contact first, but he might have done that by phone. Still, this was a sign that Freid was cracking. As long as I watched myself, I could probably still squeeze Freid a little.

As I said, that was the first incident. The second came a few hours later.

I'd eaten lunch — pizza and a cold Coke to go — and was watching Burson International when Freid walked out to his car. He wasn't carrying anything; he just got into his car and left. He waited a little longer than he should have before he pulled out onto Coit. I followed. I'd filled up with gas, and I was glad I did. We drove for more than an hour. We took I-635 around to Interstate 35, then went south to where it met Highway 67; from there we continued south to Interstate 20. We went west on 20 as if we were heading for Fort Worth, but he pulled off on Florina Road, a winding, poorly-maintained two-laner just this side of Grand Prairie. We drove through a few more streets to a new neighborhood being developed. The streets were paved, and signs were up, but most of the lots were still empty. It was going to be a nice neighborhood with lots of trees — you could see that the construction crews were taking pains to keep the trees intact instead of driving over them with bulldozers and such. I was about a hundred yards behind Freid when he went down a cul-de-sac full of wooden skeletons that would one day be houses; only, there were no construction crews finishing their jobs. I should have known better than to follow him in. It wasn't until he'd reached the end and started to turn around in the big circle that I saw a yellow truck in my rearview mirror.

Freid kept going; he hit his gas pedal when he came out of his 180-degree turn and sped past me and past the truck. I watched him take off in my mirror; as soon as he turned right and headed for greener pastures and brighter days, the truck pulled to the left, diagonally, and blocked the road. Two large guys got out.

Trouble. I kept driving forward, away from the truck and

deeper into the cul-de-sac, and then I turned around in the circle. The guys were still a couple of lots up; maybe if I just drove fast, through a few front yards, I could make good my escape.

Make good my escape? Maybe I deserved a good beating at the hands of these thugs just for using phrases like that.

But then I recognized one of the thugs. It was my own personal favorite thug — David Ben Zadok. I slowed the car to a stop, then put the transmission in Park. I got out of the car, smiling. David and the other guy — a big, muscular blond guy who didn't look like a Rhodes scholar — were nearing me. Behind them I could see the truck; set against the yellow on the door were the words "Burson International, Inc. General Contractors." They were about seventy-five feet from me when I spoke.

"You guys have a lot of work to do by yourselves," I said a little smugly. "There are, what, ten houses on this street alone. Didn't they even give you hammers?"

David looked angry. "You want hammers? We'll give you hammers."

I paused. "What's going on here?"

David's chest grew bigger; he stopped his advance toward me. He was still about sixty feet away. "What?"

"I said . . ."

"I know what you said." He held out his right arm and stopped his cohort. "You said, 'What's the Jew doing?' You have a problem? You don't like Jews?"

The other guy looked a little confused. "Hey, man, I don't think . . ."

"This guy is mine," David said. "I'll do this."

He advanced; the other guy stayed put. I was beginning to get a little worried. When David was within four feet from me he paused.

"You or him?" he asked in a low voice.

I knew what he meant. It was either bust David's cover or bust me up some. "Me," I said.

I wasn't ready for the gut-shot that came next. It was square in my diaphragm; it knocked the wind out of me and prevented me from breathing for a moment, despite the fact that breathing was something I was fond of. I heard a grunt of approval from the blond guy.

"Jim, you stay there. He now thinks I'm a Jewish pig."

I couldn't see if Jim obeyed because I was too busy getting a jab at my jaw. I was still doubled over, but I saw it coming and I made a weak attempt to block it.

"Don't block," David said softly. "I know what I'm doing. I won't hurt you."

The fact that my nerve endings were screaming in direct opposition to his statement made me reconsider my decision.

"David, you don't have to . . ."

I caught two jabs in the chest; he hit pectoral muscle (what little I have of it), reducing the chances he'd break any ribs or bruise any organs. The blows hurt, but I knew they weren't going to cause any damage.

"Go down on the next one," he said. "Close your mouth tight."

I don't know if it was his persuasive voice or the uppercut, but I obeyed. He hit me under the chin, and I stumbled backwards. I started to put my right arm back behind me, but I felt him catch the arm before I fell. He let go of it just before I hit the pavement.

"That would have broken your arm," he said, looking down at me. "Never try to catch yourself with your arm. Fall on your shoulder."

"All right!" Jim said from the background. Only he didn't sound sixty feet away. He was nearing. I turned my head and watched as he approached.

"Stop!" David ordered. Jim did so. "Throw me your knife."

I was getting even more worried now. David turned and caught a closed four-inch pocket knife Jim had thrown, then opened it with one hand. I heard a click as the blade locked into place.

"I'm going to cut you at your ear," he said softly. "Lots of blood, but little pain. It will tell Jim and Mr. Burson that I can be trusted. It will also scare Jim enough that he will want to leave and not kick you a few times himself."

I opened my mouth to protest, but another jab to the jaw, this time from David's left hand, changed my mind. The blow snapped my head back and to the side; a split second later I felt a cool breeze brush past my cheek. Then I felt something warm, and I knew it was blood from my ear, which he'd nicked like a surgeon. I raised my hand to it.

"Racist!" David snorted, then slapped at my head, forcing my hand into my ear. Blood splattered. David was right; it didn't hurt much but, boy, did it bleed.

"Now I want to see you who are," he said, loud enough for Jim to hear. I didn't know what he meant, so I just sat there and continued to bleed. David leveled a kick at me, but when he made contact he stopped the momentum and used his foot to roll me over. I complied. He reached down and took my wallet from my back pocket. I didn't resist, but then after he took it I tried to sit up. He frowned at me, and I went back down.

"Hmmm," he said, opening my wallet, "Smith. Uh, Samuel Smith. Well, Mr. Samuel Smith, take this as a warning, you are to leave Burson International people alone."

He threw my wallet at me. It hit me in the chest. He gave me one last kick — to the muscle of my thigh — then spun on his heel and started for the truck.

"Hey, man, I don't think we're supposed to kill the guy," Jim said, standing about forty feet from me. "He's a mess, man. If he dies, I didn't have nothing to do with it."

"Shut up and get in the truck, Jim," David said. "If I kill someone, you'll know it."

Jim turned and followed David into the truck. With David at the wheel, they backed up, turned around, and sped away.

For having just gotten beaten up, I looked a lot worse than I felt. I stood, checking bones; I should have had my mouth closed on that last left hook, but I'd live. I might bruise a little on my chest and thigh, but David had known what he was doing. My hand was solid red, though. I looked down, and blood was evident on my shirt. I walked to my car and opened the door with my non-bloody hand. I sat down and reached for the rearview mirror.

Jim was right; I was a bloody mess. On close inspection, it appeared that the cut was no more than one-quarter inch into my ear lobe, between the lobe and my face. I found some fast-food restaurant napkins in my glove compartment and applied pressure to the cut. It was starting to throb a little, but not as much as I would have thought.

Since my car had an automatic transmission, I was able to keep the direct pressure on the cut as I drove back one-handed to Danny's apartment. I figured my surveillance was done for the day.

At Danny's, I took off my shirt and examined the bruises that were already starting to show on my chest. I cleaned off the blood; my ear had stopped bleeding a few minutes earlier. I found a Band-Aid and stuck it on my ear and then decided to take a nap.

I was asleep on the couch when David came in; when I awoke he was sitting on the edge of the couch with a bottle of something that promised to sting and some cotton balls.

"Be still," he said. I was on my back, so he just turned my face a little, then took off the Band-Aid. "Not bad."

I don't know if he was admiring his handiwork or was glad that my injury wasn't greater. He swabbed at the cut with some-

thing on the cotton ball that did indeed sting, then came up
with a butterfly bandage that he put over the cut.

"Let's go," he said.

"Where?"

"You need a couple of stitches or it will not heal quickly. I
could do it myself — I trained as a corpsman, too — but we
should have someone do it with anesthesia."

"Yeah," I said. "Anesthesia. I like that."

David drove us to a twenty-four-hour minor emergency
clinic; for a mere $75 a doctor sewed up my ear without ask-
ing me how it got cut. He told me to clean it regularly and keep
a small Band-Aid on it.

"Do that twice a day and there will be very little scarring,"
he said. "It was a clean cut."

With the bandage on, the cut and stitches were barely visible.

When we left, I asked David about his day — the part of it
that didn't involve me.

"When we were through with you, we went to Burson's office
to report to him," David said. "We told him about Samuel
Smith."

"Samuel Smith?" I asked.

"I should give your real name? You said you met him."

"Yeah, you're right."

"So he is impressed, and he wants to keep me on hand. Jim
was scared at first, but then started bragging about how we
messed you up. And the accountant was there — Freid. He
looked worried."

"Do they know why I was bothering Freid?"

"Burson didn't seem to. He kept asking if you said anything.
And also, he asked Freid if there was a note with the flowers.
Freid said no."

"That was a lie; I wrote a perfectly nice note to go in those
flowers. Freid wasn't ready to come clean with his boss yet.
What does that mean?"

"It might mean he doesn't trust Burson. A chance we can divide and conquer later."

"That could work for us. By the way, how'd you get picked for the job of roughing me up?"

"I volunteered," David grinned. "Better me than Jim and one of his other friends. I overheard Burson talking to Jim about it. Jim works at the same site I do. So I went up and volunteered. He told us you were trying to intimidate Freid, that we should scare you off."

His tone grew more serious. "I knew I could control the situation. And you made the call."

"Yeah. You're in closer to Burson now. So what do we do? Do I get scared off or do we push Freid even harder?"

"Lay off for now. If you don't, they might start wondering about how hard a beating you really got."

"Good point. We'll let it go for a day or so. You know, we still don't know how or even if this ties in to Matt's problems."

David nodded. "Maybe they don't. Maybe we just accidentally discovered that Burson's a crook. But I doubt it."

A few minutes later Danny came in; he was a little curious about why David would want to beat me up, but he accepted our explanation.

"By the way," he said, reaching into his shirt pocket, "Julie's dad called. He said that someone named Linda Chapman has set up a meeting for 10 A.M. tomorrow. His office. He asked if you could be there."

"That's the U.S. attorney who's prosecuting Matt," I said. "I guess I can make time."

9

I was wearing an ironed shirt and a tie when I arrived at A. Vernon Robbins's office the next morning. There's no need to look sloppy for a federal prosecutor. Vernon's secretary — the same middle-aged lady who'd been with him when I was engaged to Julie — smiled as I entered.

"You can go on back," she said. "Mr. Robbins is expecting you. Care for coffee? Black, right?"

"Right," I said. I couldn't remember her name, so I avoided small talk and went straight back to A. Vernon's inner sanctum.

"I'm troubled, Emerson," he said as I entered. "All I have is a message from Linda Chapman that she's giving us one more chance to discuss the deal."

A. Vernon might have been troubled, but I kind of liked the sound of "deal."

"What deal?" I asked.

"I don't know. I never heard anything about a deal."

"How long have you been the attorney-of-record on this case?"

"A few weeks. After the indictment."

"That means a deal could have been offered before the indictment, and Matt could have turned it down?"

"I suppose. What happened to your face?"

"I got in a fight with an Israeli commando. I let him win. He has a delicate ego."

A. Vernon's eyes narrowed. He didn't like getting flippant answers, but then I wasn't getting paid. If you pay me you can expect politeness — most of the time. I ignored A. Vernon's flare. A moment later Pearl — that was her name — brought in my coffee. She brought a fresh cup for A. Vernon, doctored to perfection, I'm sure. I bet she was always polite to him, too.

"Ms. Chapman just arrived," she said. "Shall I send her back or should I give you two a few more minutes?"

"Send her back," A. Vernon said.

Pearl left, and a short, roundish, thirtyish, lawyer-looking dame walked in. She's the sort of woman who looks as if she should be called "dame" every once in a while just for good measure. Bogie would have done it. I refrained.

"Ms. Chapman, it's nice to meet you," A. Vernon said, rising. "This is Mr. Dunn, an investigator who is working on this case with me informally."

He left out the part about me being a journalist; I didn't mind. That sort of information can come in handy at unexpected moments. He also left out the part about me not being a licensed private investigator. Again, I didn't mind.

I also rose and shook Linda Chapman's hand. She had a firm grip, little makeup, and a no-nonsense attitude. She didn't question my being in the room; the defense is always allowed a lot of leeway. Still, her eyes sort of passed right over me, as if I were furniture. Investigators don't have a lot of clout in this state.

"Let's get down to business," she said, taking a seat next to me. "Last chance. Take the deal now or your client is going to prison."

A. Vernon Robbins leaned back in his overstuffed leather chair and put his hands together as if he were going to show her how to make a church, a steeple, and all the people. Instead he just made the steeple and touched his chin with it.

"Let's go over the particulars of the deal, Ms. Chapman."

"Give me Burson, and I'll give your client immunity. Those are the particulars."

I was silent; Matt wasn't even the real target. They were squeezing him to get at Burson. It made sense. Why go after Matt so hard for a paltry $200,000?

"Give you Burson how?" Robbins asked. Chapman's eyebrows started to sink toward her nose. I figured it was time to make my move.

"I can give him to you," I said. "How would you like him? Gift-wrapped? Pureed? UPS?"

She turned to look at me, paying real attention to me for the first time.

"What do you know about Burson?" she asked. I think Vernon was wanting to ask me the same thing, but he just looked curious.

Time to start winging it, I told myself. I started off with a guess. "Burson is laundering money — a great deal of it," I said. "One of the ways he did it was to route it through Matt and the church. I suspect he has several other ways, none of them large enough to draw much attention."

Chapman nodded. "But so far Matthew Hall has been the only weak link we've found to exploit."

Now she was exploiting my friend. The conversation had an impersonal feel to it; she wasn't really talking about a person, she was talking about a case.

"So where is the money coming from, and why is it dirty?" I asked.

"Where does all dirty money come from these days?"

"Drugs? I don't see it. He's a builder, not a dealer."

"Right," she said. "And what he's good at building — besides houses and government offices — are rural runways and airfields."

I paused. "Runways? What, for smugglers?"

"In areas away from large airports, so the planes won't get picked up on radar. Places like the Texas Hill Country, and on the far outskirts of the Dallas-Fort Worth area. Just big enough for small corporate jets and a few prop-planes."

"What do you need from Matt?"

"Burson is paid well for building these airstrips. We want to know where the money goes. All of it, not just the money from the church transactions."

"Easy enough. He'll know how to get that."

She turned back to A. Vernon. "We checked your client's background. He seems like a nice kid — someone who would help us. But he refused, so we pushed the indictment through. He can still walk."

"I'll approach my client with this offer," A. Vernon said without conviction. I guess maybe lawyers are trained to be that way.

I spoke up again. "And I'll approach him with a baseball bat. He'll come through. But tell me, why aren't you guys interested in Burson's scamming all these government contracts?"

Chapman smiled for the first time. Unfortunately, she was smiling at my ignorance. "Those contracts are about the only thing about him that's legitimate. He's losing money on every job he does for the government."

"Then why does he do them?"

"He doesn't mind losing a little money if it will convince the community he's an upstanding citizen. What government agency is going to suspect that their biggest contractor is building airfields for drug-smuggling?"

10

Linda Chapman had little to offer except freedom, immunity, and Matt's last chance at having a life. If it meant helping put away a guy like Deacon Willie Burson, I was all for it. After Chapman left, A. Vernon Robbins said he hoped Matt would go for it. I said I'd have a talk with Matt and that I'd use a rubber hose if necessary. I used Vernon's phone to call Matt's apartment; I left a message on his machine, asking him to drop by Danny's that night.

"I don't understand why he didn't tell me about this deal," A. Vernon said. "In a word, those terms are merciful. We'll have to make him see that."

He hadn't indicated to Chapman that he'd been completely unaware of the deal, but that was probably because he didn't want the assistant U.S. attorney to know his client hadn't been honest with him.

"I don't know why he didn't say anything about the deal before," I said. "All along, we've been working on the assumption that there was more to this than just the simple charges. We both know that Matt, like anyone else, is capable of theft. But we also both know he's not the sort to do it indiscriminately. So he's laundering money for Burson. All we have to do is get him to admit it, turn state's evidence, and he'll walk."

"Right down the aisle," Robbins said. "Remember, if he blows this, he'll be hurting Julie, too. We'll have to appeal to those sensitivities."

"I'd rather appeal to his fear of indiscriminate violence," I said. "All he had to do was tell us about this up-front."

I realized I was speaking as someone who'd been there from the beginning, instead of a last-minute consultant brought in by Robbins and Danny. But I had already invested quite a bit of vacation time and a good amount of blood in this effort.

"So what's the plan?" I asked.

A. Vernon looked amused. "The plan? You're the one who accepted Ms. Chapman's deal. The plan had better be for you to talk Matthew into helping bust Mr. Burson."

"Yeah, I guess you're right."

By lunchtime I was back at Danny's, looking through an old yearbook from college. What a bunch of nerds we were. I saw several girls I had dated; none were as pretty as Remington. In retrospect, none were as smart or as entertaining either. And none of the girls I had dated, not one, could read a baseball box score. Maybe a long-term commitment to Remington wouldn't be so bad.

I made myself a couple of sandwiches and watched a couple of talk shows on television as I waited for Danny and David to come home. I lounged on Danny's couch, and by about 4 P.M. I drifted off to sleep. Fighting crime and corruption was hard work. I woke up when I heard David come in.

"*Erev tov*," he said, Hebrew for "Good evening." "You are sleeping on the couch? I am out working in the hot sun and you are sleeping?"

"I'm sleeping off that beating I received yesterday."

David grinned. "Any bruises? Your face will get better in a few days."

"No major bruises are visible; I have a minor one on my chest and one on my leg. You can throw a punch."

David put his lunch pail on the counter and said he was going to grab a shower. "What do we have planned for tonight?"

"I hope to talk to Matt, but other than that, nothing. It's Wednesday; we could go to church with Danny."

David shrugged. He'd been to church before, with me and Remington, and it hadn't killed him. His mother would have strongly objected, I'm sure, but at the time it was necessary for safety and protection. Mine, that is. That class of junior high school kids can be rough.

"We can go if you want," David said. "I don't mind."

I nodded. "We're not finding many answers anywhere else; we might as well try there."

David shrugged again and started his shower.

Danny arrived a few minutes later and said the service started at 7:00. We ordered a pizza, and twenty-eight minutes later it arrived. We ate — I made some garlic bread to go with it — and we got ready for church. All the while I was listening for the phone to ring, hoping Matt would call. He didn't. Matt didn't show up at the door, either. While I dug out some clean slacks and a button-down shirt, David dressed in some jeans and a polo shirt. David didn't get dressed up for much.

We were literally out the door — Danny was locking it — when the telephone rang. I was past Danny and to the phone on the kitchen wall by the third ring. It was Matt.

"Things aren't hopeless, buddy," I said. "We need to talk about some things. I need to see you."

Matt paused. "When?"

"Tonight."

"We can meet at church — Danny's church — and go out for that coffee we never got," he said.

"Great."

"Emerson, I don't think it will help. There's too much at stake."

"That's what I thought about my dog."

"What?"

"Nothing — well, something . . . something complicated. It involves a chicken. But grace came down for my dog, and I think it can come down for you, too. Mercy, old buddy. It's a beautiful concept."

"Too much at stake," he repeated.

I knew better than to try to pump him for information over the phone. I didn't know what he meant about "too much at stake," but I knew I didn't have much of a chance of finding out right then. "Meet me anyway," I said.

We left for church in two cars. Danny took his truck and David, and I took David's Toyota. We arrived early enough for Danny to start his sound checks. David and I loitered toward the back, waiting for Matt. He arrived about twenty minutes before the service started, and we made small-talk until the organ got going and we had to find seats. We sat near the door (that's the first rule of journalism, by the way). After a few hymns, an associate pastor went to the podium to lead the regular Wednesday night Bible study. He was working his way through the Psalms — just as Martin was that summer — and was up to Psalm 30. He read the first three verses.

"'I will extol thee, O Lord; for thou hast lifted me up, and hast not made my foes to rejoice over me. O Lord my God, I cried unto thee, and thou hast healed me. O Lord, thou hast brought up my soul from the grave: thou hast kept me alive, that I should not go down to the pit.'

"This is a psalm of thanksgiving," the pastor said. "King David fully realizes his sin and clearly sees God's hand at work in his salvation. That sin, many feel, was probably King David's self-sufficiency in taking the census, found in 2 Samuel, chapter 24. Instead of trusting God for protection, David took a census, measuring his own strength in the number of men-at-arms he had available. Because of that sin, a plague killed seventy

thousand people, and David's strength was stripped from him.
But God's anger didn't last, nor did David's sorrow."

He went on to read the next couple of verses.

"'Sing unto the Lord, O ye saints of his, and give thanks at
the remembrance of his holiness. For his anger endureth but a
moment; in his favor is life: weeping may endure for a night,
but joy cometh in the morning.'

"In the later verses, David speaks of his pride. He returns to
the subject of the sin that brought him the sorrow in the first
place. As the psalmist goes on to say, 'And in my prosperity I
said, I shall never be moved. Lord, by thy favor thou hast made
my mountain to stand strong: thou didst hide thy face, and I
was troubled.'

"David's pride led him to believe the nation was strong
because of his leadership, but then he realized that it was by
God's grace that his 'mountain' stood strong. And when God
withheld that grace, David realized his weakness — and his
nation's weakness. And in verse 9 he makes a plea to God,
almost a legal argument, which I find interesting — 'What
profit is there in my blood, when I go down to the pit? Shall the
dust praise thee? Shall it declare thy truth?' I wouldn't try that
one in a court of law, but it seemed to work for David."

The study continued through the rest of the psalm, through
the verses of praise and worship. Something was clicking into
place.

Why *not* try that argument in a court of law? That's exactly
what I was going to attempt to convince Matt to do. If Matt
were able to give the Feds what they wanted, why would they
bother to bust him?

Immunity. What a nice word. True, I'd heard the word from
a federal prosecutor instead of from a preacher, but it still had
wonderful theological significance.

A few minutes later the service ended. David asked if he
should go on back to Danny's apartment, but I said I wanted

him to come with Matt and me. Matt looked unenthusiastic; he didn't know David well yet and didn't quite trust him.

"There's a deli a few minutes from here," Matt said after a moment of internal debate. "You two can follow me."

We left the building, found our cars, and started out of the parking lot. Matt was in the lead. He went north and east for a few miles to the Northpark area; he pulled into what turned out to be a twenty-four-hour kosher deli. There was a bar on the second floor. We parked and went in; Matt waited for us in the entryway of Levitz's New York Deli.

A waitress — no, she was probably called something else, maybe a hostess — seated us at a small, round table and gave us menus, then told us our waitress would be with us in a few moments. In the meantime, could she bring us some coffee? she asked. We all said, yes, decaf. She must have recognized his accent, or at least liked it, because when David ordered his, she smiled at him — for a little too long. After a moment she left to get our coffee.

"Oy," he said. "Beautiful. And she seems to have good taste in men."

"You're almost engaged," I said. "Remember?"

"I was only commenting. I wasn't even speculating."

The hostess (or whatever) returned and brought our coffee. She gave David his cup last. On closer inspection, I suppose I must admit David was right. She was okay, if you like the dark, mysterious, exotic, and beautiful type. "Are you Israeli?" she asked him.

"Yes," he said, grinning that dumb grin of his that women seem to love. And what an insightful answer.

"My parents just emigrated to Israel," she said. "When I have my degree, I'll probably go, too . . . if the economy picks up. It's hard to find a job there."

David nodded. She looked a little nervous, then smiled and said she'd be back to make sure everything was all right. I wondered if she meant "all right" with David personally or with our orders.

I looked at my watch; it was about 9 P.M. "Matt, let's make this quick. The Feds have offered you a deal. Why haven't you accepted?"

"It's unacceptable."

I paused. "It's not only acceptable, it's your only choice," I said, showing a little more anger than I intended. "Look, Matt, how can we help if you don't let us?"

"I didn't ask for help. I don't want help." This time Matt paused. "All I want is for you guys — and Julie, if she will listen — to know it's not as bad as it seems. *I'm* not as bad as I seem."

"What will your family think?"

"I only have my father left, Emerson, and he's not in good health. I haven't told him. I don't see a need to tell him."

"What about your pastor — Ed Aldridge? I know you were close to him in college; it appears you've stayed close . . . until lately. When I talked to him, he sounded like you're shutting him out, too."

"You talked to him?" Matt sounded a little edgy.

"Yeah. Why?"

"Leave him out of this," he said. "He doesn't need this. The church is going through some rocky times. This hasn't helped."

I suppose if any church found its finance guy was embezzling funds, the members could call those "rocky times," but I let it pass. Matt seemed more concerned about Aldridge's career path than with telling the truth to his own father. That was unexpected, but I never claimed to understand Matt. We were too different.

A waitress — a different one, one who appraised David with a disinterested eye, as if seeing whether he measured up to what her friend had said — came and took our order. I was hungry again, so I ordered steak and eggs. David had a couple of bagels with cream cheese. Matt just had coffee.

When the waitress left, I decided to push Matt a little. I knew a weak point.

"Think about Julie," I said. "This is your chance to keep from putting her through all that grief."

He didn't say anything. I was getting a little annoyed.

"Matt, they want you to turn in someone who's up to no good anyway. What possible loyalty could you have to Burson?"

"None. But I can't accept the deal. That's that."

"I'm going after him anyway, Matt."

Matt looked almost nervous. "I don't recommend that. He's dangerous. If the police get him, fine. But I can't be involved. You can't be involved either."

David spoke up. "We already are. And we're staying involved. Mr. Burson is going to jail." He said it simply, without malice or anger.

Matt looked at him. "This isn't your fight."

"It is now. I have taken difficult measures already. I will see it through. I will help Emerson. And in so doing, I think we will help you."

"Thank you, David. But no thanks."

"I think you misunderstood me. It wasn't an offer."

Matt looked at David, and David looked back. Matt was getting angry, but David showed no emotion at all.

"People could get hurt," Matt said.

"People already have," David replied. "I hurt my friend for this. Burson will not go free."

Matt stood without saying another word. He took out his wallet, removed a five dollar bill, left it on the table, and walked away.

"Something is deeply wrong with him," David said. "He's afraid."

"Of what? What could Burson do? How much muscle could

he have if he's sending new employees over to rough up a snoop like me?"

"It could be deeper . . . Not on the surface. What did the lady lawyer say about drugs?"

"Maybe you're right. She said that Burson specializes in building out-of-the-way airfields, presumably for smuggling."

"So why don't they arrest him for that?" he asked.

"I guess it's not illegal to build a private airstrip. What they're after is his drug money, I guess. That's why they're squeezing Matt. They need someone inside, in close to the books."

"Matt's not inside, is he?"

"No, but the Feds must think he can get there. I think he could, too. He just won't."

"Then that's the solution," David said.

"No, that's the problem."

"Once you find out why he won't, you can then talk him into doing it. Simple. All you have to do is find out why he wants to protect Burson."

"Right."

The hostess — true to her word — came back and asked us how everything was.

"Well, we haven't gotten our food yet," I said, although she hadn't been looking at me when she asked the question.

"It's on its way," she said. "I told them not to rush it. Actually, I wanted a chance to talk to you about Israel. I'm on break now."

Again, she wasn't looking at me, although I would have been happy to tell her everything I knew about Israel. David shrugged and motioned to a chair.

"Tell me what's it's like. Where did you grow up?"

David smiled and started talking. About fifteen minutes later, our food arrived. By the time I finished eating my steak and eggs, she was clearly in love with David.

"Yes," I said, "he even plans to take his new wife there for their honeymoon."

Her eyes got big. So did David's. "You're married?" she asked.

"Not yet," I said. "But close. Her name is Ruth. She lives in Houston."

David smiled at her while kicking me under the table. But we've got to keep each other honest. What else are friends for?

Had a coroner been present, he could have pronounced the conversation dead at that moment. The hostess — I never caught her name, but I'm sure David did — said something about her break being over. She left as quietly as Matt had.

"What is it about us tonight?" I asked. "No one wants to stay and eat with us."

"You know, now I don't mind so much that I hit you."

"Ruth would thank me if she found out. Of course, she won't find out . . . in all probability."

"You wouldn't do that — blackmail a friend."

"No, probably not. That's pretty low."

We finished our food — David hadn't actually touched his yet, but he eats fast so he was done by the time I was. The waitress came and dropped the check on our table with a smile. I dug some money out of my wallet, and David did the same.

The hostess had most probably decided that David, although unavailable, was still a nice guy, because when she saw us leaving she came over to the table.

"You guys should go on up and listen to the band," she said. "It's just a session band, but they're pretty good. The guy at the foot of the stairs is named Jerry. You guys don't need to pay the cover; I told him you were my friends."

I looked at David, and he shrugged. David, as a rule, was up for about anything. I said thanks, and we headed for the stairs. My father had instilled in me what I consider a basic principle of life: watch live musicians whenever you can. Jazz was more my father's bag than it was mine; I liked the structure of blues, a structure jazz often disposes of. Still, I was interested enough to accept her offer. We walked past a few more tables and came to the stairs. A big guy who looked like he might be named Jerry was standing there, and he smiled as he stood back and let us pass. We walked up the stairs and into a dark, relaxed bar with maybe twenty or twenty-five people in it. The bar had small round tables similar to the ones downstairs, but at the far end of the room was a stage.

And on that stage was Pete Yates, sitting behind a half-dozen mismatched drums.

He didn't see us come in. We found a table near the stage, but still in the shadows. David didn't notice him right off, so when we sat down I pointed him out. David had met Pete when Pete's band played a gig in Houston.

The session band was good. It had an acoustical guitar, a stand-up bass fiddle that looked as if it had lived a long and hard life, a French horn, and a saxophone. A woman with pretty red hair played the sax. She sat on a bar stool, to our left of the drums and Pete. The guy on bass was an older man, probably my father's age; so was the French horn player. The guitarist seemed to be about my age; he was dressed in a suit coat. They played something with a vague 1940s sound to it; it lost its historicity amid the too-modern saxophone solo currently underway. Pete played steadily, knowing it was up to the sax blower to keep within the confines of the rhythm and not the other way around.

A waitress came and asked if we wanted something to drink. We ordered more coffee, and in that moment when she stood at our table, Pete's eyes drifted over us. After a pause he turned back to me. I smiled and nodded at him; he smiled back, recognizing me. He seemed to glance at David, then back at me, and I motioned toward one of the empty chairs beside us. He smiled again and nodded. He'd come talk to us during a break.

A few minutes into the song, the guitarist stopped playing, leaving the rest to carry it. He lowered a mike stand near him, to where it was about at mid-chest level for him, and leaned down to speak into it.

"Ladies and gentlemen, Miss Rachel Cohen," he said. From behind us the hostess who had taken such an interest in David came and walked up onto the stage. She smiled at the brief applause, then nodded slightly to the rhythm, waiting for the progression to come back around. At what could only loosely be interpreted as the song's beginning, she started singing — a slow, sad World War II number about the boys who wouldn't be coming home.

I looked at David; he was watching Rachel Cohen with an emotionless face. David's usual expression was one of mild interest, even amusement. That was gone. War. He was thinking about Gershom again. I wondered how deep that wound went.

The song was apparently the end of the set; the band put down their instruments and smiled at the applause. Pete laid his sticks on the stool and came over to the table about the same time that Rachel arrived. They glanced at each other.

"You know this guy?" Pete asked her, nodding toward me.

"We've met. I was talking to his friend."

It looked as if no introductions were needed, so Pete and Rachel sat down.

"I didn't know you played here," I said to Pete.

"I'm just sitting in for a few weeks. The regular drummer got a gig in New York."

"Pete's pretty good," Rachel said. "If Murray's job turns permanent, we might hire Pete."

"What brings you guys here?" Pete asked.

"We were here with Matt," I said. "He left."

"Sort of quickly," Rachel said, looking at me.

"Yeah. I think we offended him."

Pete appeared a little concerned. "He has it rough, guys. You should go easy on him. You especially, Emerson. It's not for the likes of us to come down hard on a guy like Matt. He's a good man. At best, we're all a little shady."

"We're trying to help," I said. "But he doesn't want it."

"I know," Pete said. "Something's off. But I can't find out what it is either. He won't talk to me. He's never been like this. I've stayed close to him since college, and he's always talked to me. The only person closer was his preacher, Ed Aldridge. I guess he can't talk to him either."

Rachel must have decided against asking what this was all about. She just paid polite attention to what was said.

"He's going to get our help, regardless," I said. I turned to Rachel, who was lost by now. I didn't want to be rude, so I told her what I could.

"We have a friend who has gotten into a bit of a jam," I said. "It's just gotten more and more complicated, and he's refusing our help. We don't know why."

Rachel thought for a moment. "More and more complicated."

"Yeah."

"More and more new patterns and progressions?"

David looked a little confused, but I agreed after a moment. Those were things my father talked about. "Yeah. More and more new patterns. Progressions. They keep getting stacked on top."

"With these guys," she motioned back to the stage, "that happens a lot. When that happens I have to stop myself and go back to the original melody, concentrate on that for a while. When I'm comfortable with it again, then I'll see how it fits with everything going on top. I have to go back to the basics. Otherwise I stay lost."

"That's what we are," I said. "Lost."

"Go back to the basics," she said.

"Right. The basics. What are the basics?" I asked.

"What we know already, what we know about Matt," David said.

"Well, we know he's honest, so he wouldn't do what they said he did — get involved in a money-washing deal. Except maybe to protect someone, either himself or someone close. He's a good man."

Pete nodded. "But if he's protecting himself, we still don't know from what. And how do you protect yourself by getting yourself into legal trouble? What kind of protection is that?"

"No, stick with the basic melody," Rachel said. "You say he's honest, that he's a good man. That's your starting point. Now, what does he feel strongly about? Who or what does he love?"

"Enough to do this for?" Pete asked. "I don't know . . . Julie, certainly."

"I don't think you'll get far on that one," I said. "She didn't have access to the money, and she's genuinely confused about everything. I don't think she's involved."

"Yeah, that's right," Pete said.

"Whom else does he love?" Rachel persisted. "You guys?"

"I suppose," I said. "Us, his dad, his pastor."

I stopped cold. "His pastor. He sure wanted us to leave Ed Aldridge out of things," I said. "Could he be covering for Aldridge? Could Aldridge have taken the money?"

"Maybe," Pete said.

"I've been ignoring the rules of my own profession," I said slowly. "If someone tells me not to look under a certain rock, then the first thing I ought to do is find that rock and kick it over. So far I've been ignoring a certain rock just because someone said I should. I'll go see Aldridge tomorrow."

11

There was a single car in the church parking lot on Thursday afternoon. I'd driven by Thursday morning, but no one was there. Aldridge was probably off making his hospital rounds or something. When I went back at 2 P.M., I parked next to the old Chrysler I found close to the main entrance. No signs of extravagant spending on Aldridge's part, either. The Chrysler was easily ten years old. The main door to the church building wasn't locked, so I went through the sanctuary, which was lighted by skylights, and down the hallway to Aldridge's office. That door was open, too, and Aldridge was sitting behind his desk, just as he had been on Sunday.

"Can I help you? Oh, Mr. . . ."

"Dunn," I said.

"That's right . . . You're Matthew's friend. Have a seat. What can I do for you?"

Aldridge's coat was off, and his tie was loosened. He had four commentaries open in front of him; he appeared to be working on a text from Galatians. He took his reading glasses off and gave me his full attention. He seemed to be studying me.

"It's about Matt, of course," I said.

"Yes, of course. Is he all right?"

What a strange question. No, he's not all right, I thought. But instead I said, "I'm worried about him, as I'm sure you must be."

"Yes." Aldridge's expression didn't change.

"I don't know quite how to put this," I said. "But no one's ever said I was shy, so here it is — I don't think Matt did it. I think he's covering for someone. I think it might be you."

Aldridge's expression stayed. He paused. "What are you saying?"

"I'm saying you might have taken the money for Burson, and Matt might be trying to protect you."

Aldridge paused again. "I wish that was true. If it were, I could end this quickly and simply. I'm sorry, but it just isn't."

I studied his face; he seemed to be telling the truth. I nodded. "Okay. I think I believe you. I guess I'll go kick over a few other rocks."

"Pardon?"

"Nothing. I'm sorry to have wasted your time, and I'm sorry to have accused you."

"Not at all. You want to help Matt. So do I."

"Take my number," I said, lifting a pen from a cup full of them on his desk and writing Danny's telephone number on the back of one of my business cards. "Call me if you come across anything. Anything at all."

I grabbed one of his business cards as sort of a fair trade. Then I left the preacher in his office with his commentaries and my telephone number. I drove back to Danny's apartment, thinking about the basic melody. Matt was an uncomplicated, honest man. He was smart, good with numbers, but they weren't a passion for him. Few things were.

I got back to Danny's before 4:00. By 5:30 both he and David were home from work. David looked tired.

"It's hot," he said simply. That's a fairly safe thing to say in Texas in July.

"Is it too much?" I asked. "You don't have to keep working there, now that we know Burson's county contracts are legal."

"But if he's the target of the investigation by the prosecutor, we still might need someone inside," David said. "You want hot? You should train in a Merkava tank in the Negev Desert. I can take Dallas heat."

We ordered another pizza, then watched television for a while before going to bed — or in this case, bed, couch, and floor. Danny got a call from Paula, but he took it in the bedroom and looked a little embarrassed about the whole thing. But we were mature about it. Honest.

After the 10:00 news, we hit the sack. David lay in his sleeping bag on the floor in front of Danny's coffee table. David was out ten minutes after I turned off the light.

I lay there thinking. What Rachel had said still made sense. I knew the basics. What Matt was accused of was not something he would normally do. He was honest, hard-working, and had never even cheated on a single test that I knew of.

Still, he had admitted doing it. When I confronted Aldridge, I assumed Matt hadn't taken the money for Burson. I was wrong.

Back to the basics.

Embezzling wasn't something Matt would normally do. But would he take the money for Burson in a situation that wasn't normal? Maybe our original gut-feeling last night was right; maybe he was protecting someone. I had assumed he was protecting the person who had really done it, and Aldridge certainly had the opportunity. But what if he was protecting someone from something else?

Suddenly I thought of what David had said before: "you wouldn't blackmail a friend, would you?"

There are actually very few motives for someone like Matt to commit a felony — for any of us to commit a crime, for that matter. Greed, lust, and fear. When narcotics and mental instability (factors that remove any and all sense from a crime) aren't involved, most crimes can be put into one of those three categories.

Greed — that was out. Matt simply wasn't greedy; and besides, Burson was the one gaining from the operation. The prosecutor hadn't said anything about Matt taking a cut.

Lust — that was out, too. Julie was on the outside of this. I didn't know of any other women, but I knew Matt. That wouldn't be like him.

But fear — that's the key. If he was afraid — not for himself, but for someone he loved — would he do it? Yes. Most of us would.

And blackmail seemed a likely motive. Burson didn't have a gun to Julie's head, nor to Aldridge's. So it must have been information. Julie was simply too young to have been in too much trouble so far, I felt, but Aldridge wasn't. I was back to the basics of my own profession — kicking over rocks someone had told me to leave alone.

I turned the lamp back on. David groaned. I found the shirt I had been wearing; Aldridge's card was in the pocket. His home phone was on the front of the card, printed just below his office number. I figured if he had his home number on his card, he must want me to call, right?

I went to the telephone on the wall in the kitchen and dialed the number. Aldridge answered on the second ring; he didn't sound asleep.

"I don't want to sound impolite, but is there anything else you've done?" I asked after I identified myself.

Aldridge didn't respond.

"This is for Matt," I said. "If someone knows something that could hurt you, Matt might be doing this to protect you. Is there anything Burson could have found out?"

Again, Aldridge didn't answer for a moment. Then he

responded slowly, "Maybe so. Meet me at the church in the morning. We can talk about it then."

"Fine. How's 10:00?"

"I'll be there."

As I hung up I felt a little uneasy about giving him an extra few hours. When you blindside someone with a question such as "What terrible things are there in your past that could be used against you?" you usually want their first response. The more they think about things, the more they'll explain away to themselves the really juicy stuff. When Wally, a political candidate I knew, had asked me if he should run for office the first time, I asked him that question. Better it was me in an informal setting than one of his opponents during a public debate.

Aldridge had time to think about it; still, I had faith that deep down he wanted to help Matt.

I went back to the couch and went to sleep. I dreamed about Remington again. This time Airborne was in the dream too.

When we woke up the next morning, we made some loose plans for the evening. Danny had a date with Paula, and this time we weren't invited. I said I'd buy David some dinner to make it up to him. He mentioned Levitz's New York Deli, but I said I'd have to check with Ruth on that.

David and Danny left for work, but I watched a news program while I waited until it was time to see Aldridge. At 9:30 I left the apartment and headed for West Dallas. I pulled into the church parking lot just after 10:10; the traffic had been a little heavy.

I walked into Aldridge's office and stopped immediately at what I saw. Aldridge, glancing up at me, looked as if his best friend had just been shot, stabbed, poisoned, hit by a train, and slandered. Aldridge obviously hadn't slept the night before; he was wearing a suit that was clean and pressed, but he hadn't shaved.

He motioned for me to sit down. Without saying anything he handed me a newspaper clipping.

UNIDENTIFIED MAN SHOT

New Orleans — An unidentified man remains in critical condition at New Orleans Memorial Hospital today, after suffering a gunshot wound late last night.

The victim was brought to the hospital by a cab driver, who said he found the man leaning against a lamppost on Bourbon Street.

Police say no identification was found on the man, and they're waiting for him to regain consciousness before continuing their investigation.

I looked up at Aldridge. "Tell me about it."

"It happened twelve years ago," he said. "I was in school — New Orleans Baptist Seminary. A group of us would go to Bourbon Street for street evangelism every week. During winter, when it got cold, the group would dwindle. Sometimes it was just me. Bourbon Street got pretty scary late at night; when I was alone once, I thought a man was going to rob me. So I started bringing a gun with me when I went by myself. I knew it was wrong, but I was afraid. And one night a man approached me. It was cold and raining; I was standing under an awning. I was about to go home. No one was out. It was in January, a few weeks before Mardi Gras. The man was the only other person I could see. He came to me and asked me for some money. I told him it wasn't money I had to offer; I started my speech, but he was angry. He was drunk. He started yelling at me, getting angrier and angrier. He tried to take my Bible, he was yelling something about what Jesus said about the poor, and I panicked. I took the gun from my coat just to scare him, but I shot him. I thought he was going to kill me. Instead, I think I killed him."

"And you didn't call the police."

"No. I ran. I just went to my car and left."

"Did he die?"

"I don't know," the pastor said. He looked old. "I tried to find out, but I couldn't. The newspapers dropped the story before his name was released."

"It's a pretty small item," I said. "That clipping is just from the police blotter. But don't underestimate us journalists, Ed — eh, Mr. Aldridge. If the guy had died, chances are, the newspaper would have reported it."

I thought for a moment. This could be it. "Does Willie Burson know about this?"

"Willie?" Aldridge looked a little confused. "Why?"

"Does he?" I pressed.

Aldridge paused. "He knows. He was the chairman of the Pastor Search Committee. When they flew me out to Texas, I stayed in a hotel. I called Willie to my room the Sunday night after I preached. I told him; he said he'd pray about it. The next day he said we wouldn't mention it to the committee or to the church. He said God had forgiven me, so it shouldn't be held against me."

"That was the wrong thing to do, I think."

"You're in the business of right and wrong?" Aldridge looked a little resentful.

I smiled. "In a manner of speaking, yes, I am. I'm not telling you anything you don't know. You realize you had more responsibility than that to the guy you shot."

"Yes."

"Now, does Matt know?"

"Yes."

"How?" This was tougher than trying to get information from a lawyer.

"I went to New Orleans three years ago," he said. "It had been eating at me. It still is. I went to go through the newspapers, to see if I could find out anything about the man. I told Matt I was going to see some friends from seminary. I made up some names. Matt tried to contact me; when I returned, he asked me about that. I told him the truth. He said he wouldn't do anything to hurt my ministry."

As if he'd hit upon something — anything — he could use in his defense, Aldridge looked up at me with a hint of desperation in his expression and tone.

"My ministry," he said, "that's what's important. Not me, not what I've done, not the past, but what I'm doing for God now."

I shook my head. I wasn't in the business of offering absolution. "You know better than that."

He dropped his eyes from mine and nodded slowly. "What will we do?"

"Well, we simply have to clear this thing up," I said. "We don't know what happened to the victim, but we can find out."

I thought I saw a faint light of hope in Aldridge's face. He nodded again.

"And then you're going to have to go public," I said. "I think Willie Burson, your deacon, is blackmailing Matt with the information. The only way to solve this is a preemptive strike — do what Burson is threatening to do."

Aldridge looked confused. "Willie?"

"He's dirty," I said. "Don't confront him, don't let on like you know. But soon, from the pulpit, you've got to confess."

"Sunday?" he asked.

"No. I've got to get Matt inside close to Burson's books. Hold off on it. I'll tell you when."

"But how will we know about the man I shot?"

"Let me make a quick telephone call."

I took the phone and dialed the direct number to Detective Sergeant Bill Singer's office. He answered immediately. "Police. Singer."

"It's Emerson," I said. "I need a favor."

"Gee, that's new. Are you back in town?"

"No, I'm in Dallas. Listen . . . About twelve years ago, on January . . ."

I looked at Aldridge. "The 9th," he said.

"On January 9th twelve years ago a guy was shot in New Orleans . . . On Bourbon Street. He was taken to New Orleans Memorial Hospital, and the last we heard he was in critical condition. All I need to know is whether he died and if any charges were filed in the case."

"Do you have a name?"

"I knew you were going to ask me that. No, we don't. Sorry. But I know you can do this. You're a detective."

"You owe me big. I suppose you need this yesterday."

"As soon as you can get it, buddy."

"If you call me buddy again I'll arrest you. Give me a telephone number. I'll see what I can dig up. I have some contacts in the New Orleans police department."

I gave him the phone numbers for Aldridge's office and Danny's apartment.

"Fine," he said. "But call me later today if you haven't heard from me. And, Dunn, you owe me big."

"I know."

I hung up. "That was a cop friend of mine," I said. "He'll look into it."

Aldridge nodded.

"Now remember," I added, "don't say anything to Burson."

"He's one of my most trusted friends."

"Then you've got to develop better taste in friends. Just promise you won't say anything to anybody."

"Fine."

"I'll let you know as soon as I know anything. If Singer calls here, take a message for me. He'll probably say something cryptic and coded, like 'Yeah, the guy's a stiff,' or 'Bad shot, he lived.' Tell Singer I'll call him later."

"Thank you."

"Yeah."

I left the building and drove north to Julie's apartment. I didn't know if she would be home, but it was Friday and she didn't work Fridays. She answered when I knocked. She looked tired and as if she'd just gotten out of bed; it was already noon. She still looked good, however, in jeans and a sweatshirt.

"Come on in," she said. "Making any progress?"

"I think so," I said, stepping into her apartment. "Are you going to talk to Matt today?"

"Sure. Why?"

"Just wondering. I'll need to see him. But it's not urgent."

We walked into her sci-fi living room, and she sat down, assuming I'd do the same without invitation. I did.

"What brings you here?"

"I think I've got it figured out," I said. "I know why Matt did what he did. And if we work hard, we can still get him out of trouble. It means he'll have to work with the Feds. I'm going to need your help. So far he hasn't been easy to convince."

"What makes you think he'll listen to me?"

I paused. "Because you love him and he knows it."

She didn't say anything. She was sitting on the greenish, formless couch, cross-legged and small. She was studying one of her shoes. I studied her. My initial impression was right. Her hair was a bit disheveled; she had no makeup on; she wore her sneakers without socks. She'd been up for a short while at best. I sighed and got up.

"Coffee?" I asked. "I'll make it."

"Sure."

I found my way into her kitchen; it was small, like most apartment kitchens. On the counter was a familiar coffee maker; I'd given it to her for Christmas a couple of years ago. In the cupboard above the coffee maker I found the filters, and the coffee was in a plastic container in the freezer. She didn't use whole beans; probably too much effort for mornings. Julie was never a morning person.

As I measured out the coffee, I talked to her over the counter that faced out into the living room. "How was work this week?"

"Fine. I'm getting tired of that job, though. My dad wants me to go to paralegal school and come work for him."

"You'd like that."

"Maybe. Couldn't be worse than what I'm doing now. I feel brain-dead. It's mindless, just typing all day."

"It still pays well. Better than journalism. Think they'd give me your old job?"

She didn't respond to that. I hit the On button, went back into the living room, and resumed my place on a chair facing the couch.

"Julie, if Matt doesn't want any help, and if he does go to jail for this, would you stay with him or would you break it off?"

She was now staring at some miniscule smudge on her glass-topped coffee table; it took her a moment to speak. She didn't look up at me when she did.

"I guess that's what you would think of me. Julie Robbins, well, she's okay, except she's not very loyal. You want loyal, get a dog.'"

"I've got a dog, remember? He likes my girlfriend more than he likes me."

She smiled. "Yeah, I remember your dog." And again she paused, seemingly to collect her thoughts. But her thoughts were apparently summed up in one word. "Yeah."

"Yeah, what?" I asked. I had forgotten the question.

"I'd stand by my man," she said with a put-on country twang, still looking at her coffee table. She was smiling. "I know you think I wasn't very faithful before, but it's not that simple."

"It never is."

She shook her head, still not looking at me. "How long ago was that, anyway?"

"Which part?" I asked.

"When did you leave?"

"I got the job and went to work, what, two and a half years ago. Seems like longer. And then you broke off the engagement about a year after that. It was winter, as I recall. We'd made it through the tough part; we only had part of a semester left before you were out of school."

"You're still mad about it . . . hurt."

"No, I don't think so, just curious. You never really told me why."

"Where's that coffee?" she asked. Obviously she had no intention of telling me why now.

I got up and fixed two cups. Julie liked both cream and sugar, while I drank it black. That could be the reason for the whole breakup, but I sort of doubted it. I brought her coffee to her and put it on the glass-topped table. She mumbled something to the effect of "thanks" and looked at the cup instead of the spot on the table. At least I was adding a little variety to her life.

I took a sip of my coffee. It was too hot to enjoy, but it gave me an excuse for having nothing to say.

"Tell me about your new girlfriend," Julie said after a moment.

"Okay," I said. "She's about so tall, kinda pushy, and very smart."

"Is she pretty?"

"Yeah. Dark hair, blue eyes. And she's fun. Good pitching arm."

"Where did she grow up?"

"Houston. Her parents were divorced when she was younger; she lived with her mother, mostly."

"Has she ever let you down?"

I frowned. Where was this train of thought scheduled to derail? I wondered. "I suppose she has . . . Sometimes . . . Nothing big."

"Could she let you down big? How far could she go? If she got in trouble, would you leave her?"

Ah. I saw where she was going with this. Matt. "No, I wouldn't leave her," I said slowly. "Ever, I guess. How far are you going to push me on this topic?"

She smiled and looked at me for the first time since she'd sat down. "Keep going," she said. "I want to hear it. You ignore your feelings, Emerson, you always did. Until I made you talk about them. Tell me about her."

"Well, if she got into the kind of trouble Matt's in, I think I'd probably figure that the trouble was a symptom and not the sickness itself," I said. "In which case, she'd need me to help her get well. Matt's like that. He's not a bad man, he's just ill . . . In the soul. And in this case, the sickness didn't start with him, he just sort of caught it, just like you always caught whatever virus was going around the dorm, remember?"

"Go on."

"Maybe *sickness* isn't the right word for this. Maybe *splinter*. Maybe a federal grand jury indictment is kind of big for a splinter, but you get the idea. The first thing we've got to do is get the splinter out, then we can concentrate on healing."

"And you want me to help."

"Right. Tell Matt to come over after work; you and I will gang up on him. We've got to talk him into cooperating with the prosecutor. They don't really want Matt."

"They don't?"

"No. I'm surprised your father didn't tell you. They want Willie Burson. They'll let Matt off, but only if he delivers Burson on a plate."

"All this is to protect Willie Burson?"

"No, I think it's all been to protect someone else."

Julie's eyes clouded over. "I'll call him. But why haven't you given up? Matt told me about your conversation in the car. You said you never particularly liked him. He said he told you the same thing."

"I guess that's the gist of what was said. But you have to understand, it's not whether I liked or disliked him. It's more than that between the four of us. It always has been. I don't know if I can explain it."

"Are you going to use the 'guy thing' excuse?"

I laughed. "Not now, I won't. No, that wouldn't explain it. It's like this: a friendship is something more than a moment-to-moment opinion of someone, you know? You don't always like your family members; that doesn't change the fact that they're family. Matt's sort of family to me; they all are — Danny, Matt, Pete. For now and forever, if those nerds get into any trouble, I'll be around to help get them out. I think they'd do the same for me. We lived together for a year — longer if you count living down the hall from each other in the dorms. That builds a bond of some kind. The house we had was a residence of convenience at first, but now I guess I see it was more than that. Maybe God was putting us together, binding us together for future situations such as this."

"Hmmm." She reached over and picked up a cordless phone that had been sitting on the floor beside the shapeless couch. I hadn't noticed it was there. She dialed a number, asked for Matt, then after a moment told him she needed to see him right after work. I thought she made it sound a little melodramatic, but it worked. She smiled and told him she loved him. I did a quick spot-check for pangs of regret or anything of that nature, but there was nothing worth mentioning.

"He'll be over at about 5:30," she said. "It's Friday; he usually takes off a little early on Fridays, but the traffic's pretty bad. Do you want to wait here?"

"I guess so; I might run out and get a newspaper."

"Okay," she said. "I'll be here. You can pick up a couple of burritos for lunch, if you want."

Julie always did have a way of making me buy her food.

"Sure," I said. I let myself out, and I heard her lock the door behind me. I drove a few blocks to a convenience store and found a Dallas paper. That reminded me that I hadn't called Doug Chen lately. I made a note to do it later that afternoon. I then wandered through the streets in my ancient car searching for a Mexican fast-food place. After about twenty minutes I found something that offered seriously Americanized burritos. I bought several, as well as some soft drinks, and headed back to Julie's apartment.

Her hair was in a towel when she answered the door. She let me in and said she was going to dry her hair before she ate. I went to her kitchen table and spread out the newspaper. I checked the sports section.

I almost fainted; the Rangers were only two games back in the American League West division. They had a game scheduled for that night, against the Brewers. David was going to get to see a game, after all. I called the ticket office and found out that there were still almost ten thousand seats left, so I knew we could get in on short notice. When Julie came out of the bathroom, I asked her if she and Matt wanted to catch the game with me and David.

"Emerson, I haven't changed that much," she said. "Baseball is boring. They just stand around and spit . . . and do other things."

I shook my head sadly. "Someday, Julie my dear, you will see the light. Baseball is a microcosm of life, a carefully choreographed dance, a portrait of all that we love and strive for and cherish. Except in real life it's tougher to find a decent hot dog."

"You never change. Gimme a burrito."

I fed the girl, as I was supposed to, despite the fact that she was obviously wandering about in a sort of fog. Is anything more beautiful than a triple play with that final tag at home plate? Anything more poetic than a split-fingered fastball? I think not.

After we ate we talked some more about the year and a half since we'd broken up. She asked about my job, and I asked about hers.

At about 4:00 I called Detective Sergeant Bill Singer, hoping he had heard something.

"Your victim was one Walter S. White," Singer said. "That case was never closed by the New Orleans PD, but it should have been. Mr. White died eight months later from multiple gunshot wounds."

"So my guy killed him . . . Wait — eight months later?"

"Right. He recovered fine from the single gunshot wound to the abdomen in January; he was released from the hospital four days later. And eight months after that, in an altercation with an alleged drug dealer, he was plugged. He couldn't remember anything about the first shooting; he was too drunk at the time, according to the statement he gave to officers."

"What's that mean? I've got the guy who did the first shooting. Should he turn himself in? He doesn't have any priors; I think he could probably get probation."

Singer laughed. "He'd only make the district attorney mad. The DA would have to exhume a twelve-year-old aggravated assault case when he's got two-a-day murders to worry about. Let it alone. No one's going to come knocking on your guy's door. The victim and only witness is dead. File closed."

"Great. I'll tell him."

"You'll make this up to me soon, won't you?"

"Of course," I said. "Have faith."

I hung up and dialed the office number on Aldridge's business card. "You're clear," I said when he answered.

I told him about Mr. White, his untimely and inconvenient death, and the DA's likely reluctance to prosecute a case with an exemplary defendant, a dead victim, and no witnesses. I told him it was over.

"What does this mean?" he asked.

"It means that if I'm right, and Burson is using this to make Matt take a dive in his behalf, the game just went into extra innings."

All right, all right, I realize there's a rule somewhere about mixing metaphors, especially sports metaphors, but no one's perfect.

Aldridge didn't comment on my poor grammar; he didn't even comment on the judgment that had just been lifted from his shoulders and the mercy he'd been shown. He was quiet; I started to wonder if he was still on the line. After a moment, though, he spoke.

"Emerson, when will you confront Burson?"

"I don't know. I have a plan forming, though. I'll let you know. But don't say anything to anyone yet."

"Thank you."

"Sure."

As I hung up I looked at Julie; she was pale. "You have a plan for Burson?"

"No, I said I had a plan forming. It's an interesting process; sort of like the way the orange juice in your refrigerator has gotten thicker and thicker over the past few months, to the degree that it's now quite solid."

She ignored my editorial comment on her housekeeping habits. "What about Matt?" she asked.

"He'll be here in a few minutes; we'll talk about it then."

She nodded. I read some more of the paper; then at 5:00 I turned on the early news. Nothing important; the weather guy said it would be a hot night, and the sports guy said the Rangers had a good chance of winning tonight against Milwaukee.

By 5:30 I was getting impatient. The national news came on.

At 5:37 Matt walked in. He looked hot; he was carrying his suit coat instead of wearing it.

"Hello, Matt." He was surprised to see me. If he was worried I was there to steal Julie back, he didn't show it. He came and shook my hand.

"Sit down, Matt," Julie said. "Emerson wants to talk to you."

Matt knew what was coming. He made that clear with a sigh and the reluctant way he took a seat on the couch near — but not too near — Julie.

"I've already told you you're wasting your time," he said.

"I don't think I am," I said. "Now be quiet and listen. I know about Aldridge."

His expression didn't change; he still looked tired and a little bored.

"What about Aldridge?"

"I know about the shooting in New Orleans. Matt, he didn't kill the guy. But someone else did, a few months later. No victim, no witnesses, no crime. The DA has enough to worry about; he's not going to come after Aldridge, even if Aldridge goes public with it."

Matt began to look interested. "Goes public with it?"

"To get you off the hook, Matt. I know about Burson, too. I know about the airfields, and I know about the money laundering. I know that if you work with the federal prosecutor, you won't have to throw your life away. How many accountants do you think they really want or need in a federal prison?"

"Dunn, I'm serious this time — *stay away*," he said. He sounded serious. Serious enough that he stood up. His face was turning red. "This is none of your business. I think you should go home. Leave Dallas . . . And leave me alone. I don't need your help, and I'm not working with the prosecutor. I did exactly what they said I did, and I'm ready to accept the penalty. Just leave. Now . . . Please."

He motioned at the door with his head. I looked at Julie. She was staring at the floor.

"Fine, Matt," I said. "That's fine with me."

I left the apartment without saying anything more, which is saying a lot. I wanted to throttle Matt, but it was his life. I had a ball game to attend.

Matt's anger was digging at me. The more he wanted me to leave things alone, the more I wanted to ignore his advice. It was not a matter of patience or steadfastness; it was stubbornness. I didn't want to go home having failed to help a friend.

I thought about Matt and Aldridge as I drove to Danny's. I was wrong. Matt wasn't protecting Aldridge; not that Aldridge didn't need protecting. I wondered about the question I'd asked the pastor: "What have you done?" I laughed out loud as I was driving. What if someone asked me that? What if someone asked any of us that? Wouldn't we all have something — some secret sin — that we had kept buried, afraid someone would find out? What a question to ask a nice guy like Aldridge. Or me. Especially me.

It was after 6 P.M. when I arrived at Danny's apartment. David's car was there; Danny's wasn't. I went in and found David asleep on the couch. It had been a rough week for the poor guy; a week of effort wasted, now that Matt had refused the last offer of help and thrown me out of someone else's apartment. I wasn't too worried about the rejection. I've been rejected by better people than him and thrown out of better places than that apartment.

David stirred when I entered. "David, I'm going to make it all up to you. I'm taking you to a Rangers game."

"Okay." He leaned up on the couch and searched for his watch. He found it on his arm. "Yeah, okay."

David wasn't a hard guy to convince.

We had a little more than an hour to get across town to Arlington Stadium, that tabernacle of mediocre teamwork.

David had already taken a shower, so I changed, and we left in his Toyota. We parked about half a mile from the stadium, walked to the ticket counter, and bought outfield bleacher seats. Sure, we could have afforded fancy infield seats that had backs and padding, but what fun would that be? Ruben Sierra was about thirty feet away, patrolling the outfield slowly like an old beat cop. The teams were already two outs into the first inning when we sat down; the game was off to a quick start. Some new kid was pitching for the Rangers. I didn't recognize the Brewer at bat.

"You think this is the same umpire as before . . . ?" David inquired.

"I don't think so," I said. "But don't worry, he can't see us from way over there anyway."

"Good. I don't like him already. That last pitch wasn't a strike. Hey, ump, get your glasses!"

David started laughing as if he'd said something the umpire hadn't heard before. A gray-haired black man in front of us turned around to David and nodded solemnly. "That's right, son. That weren't no strike. I could see from here it was at his ankles."

For the next two innings David and the black man yelled almost in unison. By the third inning the guy, whose name was James, had moved one row up, right next to David. We were all sharing a bag of peanuts and creating a wonderful mess with the shells. James was a preacher, he said, at the Jerusalem A.M.E. Church. David turned to the man in serious doubt. "You're from Jerusalem?"

The preacher laughed. "That's just the name of the church. You sound like you might be from there, though."

"I'm from Haifa," David said. "It's near Tel Aviv. I worked in Jerusalem some."

David found it easy to make friends; when the two weren't talking about the Holy Land, which James had always wanted to see, they were criticizing the umpire and the general behavior of the Milwaukee Brewers.

In the fourth inning we had hot dogs. The Rangers were trailing 3-0, and I was starting to get depressed about that, and also about Matt.

"It's timing," James said, leaning around David and addressing me. "It's all in the timing."

I nodded.

"Baseball is a mental sport," James said. "If the pitcher hesitates too long between throws, or if the runner at first takes off a little too early, the other team can sense the desperation. But if the timing is just right, if the pitcher shows some confidence to the batter, if the runner shows some guts, this here game can be turned around. Timing," James added. "Timing."

And then came the streak. Thwack. Thwack. Thwack. With three pitches, all strikes, a Brewers batter was sent home early. One curve and two fastballs.

Another batter stepped up. Windup. Heat — a fastball. Thwack. Breaking ball. Thwack. Heat. Thwack. Another batter down and out in what was turning into an interesting game.

The third batter approached; we could see his lips moving. He was saying something rude to the catcher, no doubt. The kid at the mound was doing all right. Two up, two down, six pitches. He went into his windup. Fastball. Thwack. Fastball. Thwack. Slider. Thwack. The batter went down swinging at something that wasn't there. It was beautiful. An almost unheard-of streak.

Timing. Nine pitches, nine strikes. Beautiful.

Julie Robbins.

"David . . ." I said. But I couldn't say anything more. The thought was suffocating. What if Matt had been protecting Julie? I went through the chronology in my head. The breakup. Her job. A time lapse. Months unaccounted for. The math was right.

David looked over at me. "Emerson? You okay?"

"David, what if it was Julie? What if Matt has been protecting Julie?"

"What could she have done?"

James was looking at us with curiosity. I didn't care.

"She was out of circulation for six months," I said. "Out of school early, at home. No one saw her. She didn't finish that last semester until a year later."

David wasn't slow; his eyes widened. "Yours?"

I laughed without humor. "No. No way."

"Good. Remington will be glad to hear that."

"Yeah. What do I do?"

He shrugged. "We ask her, I suppose. We get her side of it. Are you sure about it?"

"No. But it adds up."

David shrugged again. "Then don't worry about it now. Watch the ball game."

I nodded and turned my attention back to the game. Sierra must have appreciated our support for his team and our constant badgering of the umpire, because he sent a long, sailing homer out to our side of the stands. A kid four rows down and about thirty feet over caught the ball.

For the rest of the game I went over the math in my head again and again. The breakup was swift and without warning. It came on a February afternoon. She left school soon after that. No word from her until late July, according to Danny. She didn't start back at school until the next January; she finished her degree in May, a year late. Long enough to have a child and recover, even lose most of the weight she'd probably gained. Then she started dating Matt.

The Rangers pulled it out, surprisingly. They beat the Brewers 5-4. When the game ended, James handed David and me each a business card.

"If you boys need anything, here's where to find me," he said.

"And next time you're in town and want to see a ball game, call me. I'll buy the peanuts."

It took us forty-five minutes to get out of the parking lot. We found our way onto Interstate 30 and started east toward Danny's apartment.

"I guess this means we don't go home tomorrow?" David asked.

"No, I guess not. We'll stay a few more days . . . See what we can do. I've never worked this hard to help anyone who was as completely unappreciative, though."

David frowned at me. "Is that why you do it?"

"What do you mean?"

"You help someone because of who they are or how they respond?"

"I guess . . . I don't know."

"That's not right."

"What do you mean?" I repeated.

"I mean, we should help Matt because of who *we* are — we are his friends — rather than who or what he is — which is a jerk, right now. Remember Jesus?"

I laughed. "I think so."

"When He healed the ten lepers? And only one appreciated it? What about the nine others? He didn't heal them because they were nice guys and would thank Him; He knew they wouldn't. He healed them because of who He was."

"David, what are you saying? Have you been reading that New Testament I gave you?"

"Some."

"Yeah? What do you think?"

"I think I'm still reading."

"Let me know if you have any questions."

"I will."

I was a little surprised, but I didn't push him. "You're right, though."

"I know," he said. "I keep telling you that. You should listen to me more often."

I ignored that. "We're Matt's friends, so we should keep him out of jail whether he likes it or not."

"Right. Now, what about Julie?"

"We find out if it's true. If it is, we go from there."

"That's a very detailed plan. Did you think it up all by yourself?"

"Nobody asked you," I said with a laugh. "Just follow my directions. We might as well go see Julie and Matt now."

I told him how to get to Julie's apartment. Then another thought struck me. What if it was Matt? I dismissed it immediately. They hadn't started dating until later. And Matt wasn't the type.

But neither was Julie. How could something like that happen? Why was I even suspicious? In the daylight, the thought would be ridiculous. But I thought of Julie alone up in Dallas while I was stuck in a small town south of Houston; I thought of the loneliness she must have felt. I had told myself I had no choice. I was ahead of Julie in school, and when I got the job offer from Barney, I couldn't turn it down. The number of graduates getting jobs in the journalism field was pretty slim, I told her. I was lucky to get the opportunity.

She wanted me to hold out for something in Dallas. But with no experience and a degree from a small college, the big Dallas paper wouldn't look twice at me, I knew. And the other, smaller papers were laying off, not hiring.

So she helped me move my stuff down to the shabby apartment that I'd recently left. She hated the apartment. She hated the town. She would have been miserable, and I knew it. I told myself that when we got married I'd look for something closer to the city.

When she broke the engagement I was hurt. Maybe too hurt

to look for reasons. She said it was because she'd started dating someone else. That wasn't like her, but I didn't question it.

I was numb for months. I didn't start dating again for more than a year. Remington had pulled me out of a slump. But I had never bothered to go back and look at what had thrown me into that slump in the first place.

David asked me to point out the right apartment complex as we neared it.

"There," I said. Then I directed him to Julie's apartment. We parked.

"Here goes," I said profoundly. We walked up to her door and knocked. Matt answered.

"What?" he said, equally profoundly.

"I wanna talk," I said.

He shrugged and let us in. Julie was reading a book on the couch; a *Wall Street Journal* was open on the coffee table. A quiet evening at home.

"Hello, Julie," I said. "Were you pregnant?"

She looked up with surprise in her eyes. I felt a hand on my shoulder. I was spun around, and I saw little except Matt's fist coming at my face. As I was contemplating the ramifications of that sight, it hit. I felt pain, I lost sight for a few seconds, but I didn't feel any cartilage in my nose go east for the winter. Still, this was not good. Not good at all, actually. Brewers 1, Rangers 0.

My knees were buckling, and I was starting to go down. I saw Matt reaching back, but then I saw David catch his arm at the same time that my favorite photographer caught me around the waist. He held me up for a second until I regained my footing.

"Watch it," I said to Matt. "He gets mad when anyone does that to me but him."

Why was I getting beaten up by all my friends lately? Was this a sign to rethink my brand of cologne or something?

To my right there were a few spots of blood on Julie's nice, light-colored carpet. I said I was sorry. David had let go of me, but was still holding Matt's forearm and staring deeply into Matt's eyes. David had no expression; he just 'stared. Matt relaxed a little, so David let go of his arm. David then turned to me. With his thumbs he massaged my nose for a moment of excruciating pain. "Not broken," he said.

"I could have told you that," I said.

David's hands were a little bloody; he reached over to a box of tissues on the end table next to the couch and grabbed a handful. He gave them to me, and I held them up to my nose.

"Yes." It was Julie's voice. I'd almost forgotten that I had asked a question.

We all turned to Julie.

"You don't have to say anything, Julie," Matt said.

"I know. But he's right. Yes. I was . . . in trouble."

"Tell me about it."

Matt shook his head and went over to the couch. "Don't, Julie."

"I want to. He has a right to know. It wasn't his fault. None of it was. Emerson, I'm sorry. During Christmas break that year I met a guy. I was lonely, and there were all these parties to go to, and you could never come. So he took me out . . . a lot. Things happened, things that never happened between us, and in January I started getting sick . . . in the mornings. I went to the health clinic at school; the nurse told me I was pregnant. I went to our pastor for counseling. He talked with my father, and they got in touch with a family who wanted to adopt."

Julie was crying now. "I was in love with you, Emerson, but I died then. I dropped out of school. I went home and was by myself day after day, watching myself grow bigger and bigger because of a stupid mistake — a wrong choice. The old Julie died slowly. When I gave away that little girl, I gave away the last thing that was left of me. And then Matt came. He — he helped rebuild me. I started going to church again. I finished school."

I nodded, still holding the tissues to my nose. "We could have kept the child," I said.

"That's easy to say now. Would you have said it then? I kept waiting for the phone to ring, Emerson. You didn't make any effort to get me back. You never called to ask why. You must not have thought I was worth the extra effort."

I nodded. That's me — that's the kind of mistake I would make, the kind that would hurt someone else the most. "Where is she?" I asked softly. I wasn't sure I wanted to know.

"Austin. I haven't seen her since. I think about her every day." She continued to cry. I searched my own soul for any feelings; I found nothing but confusion. A child? A little girl? Would I have married Julie anyway? I didn't know.

"Forgive me, Julie," I said. "I'm sorry. I should have seen it — I should have seen something."

Julie didn't respond for a moment; after a pause, she nodded.

David reached over and gently leaned my head back and moved my hands away from my face.

"The bleeding has stopped. But keep a tissue handy."

"Whatever you say." Back to business. I turned to Matt. "That's it, isn't it? You're protecting Julie. How did Burson know?"

"I don't know."

"I do," I said. "It's probably pretty common for a pastor — right or wrong — to take this sort of problem to the chairman of the deacons."

"Maybe." Matt sounded dull. He was sitting beside Julie and had put his arm around her.

"And what has Burson said? That he'll tell the church about it?"

Julie looked up at Matt. It was clear she didn't know about the blackmail.

"Think of what it would do to her, Emerson," Matt said, looking at Julie and not at me. "Reliving it every time she saw somebody whisper."

"Is that why you're going to jail?" Julie said to him. "I lost my baby, and now I'm going to lose you? You can't. You can't do that to me. You have to do what Emerson says!"

She said it with less of a commanding tone than an imploring one. She looked straight into Matt's eyes as she said it. He started to argue.

"Shush," she said. "You will not leave me. You will not ruin my future. My past is already ruined; let them say what they want. I'm not the first."

"I think I have to agree, Matt," I said. "I don't think your wanting to protect Julie is wrong, but I think your pride is also involved here."

Matt found nothing to say. He looked up at me. Julie spoke up.

"You're a proud man, Matt," she said, "and you know it. You've always been careful to keep it under control, to not let it hurt anyone. Well, it's hurting someone now. Me. I don't want to lose you. I can't lose you. Listen to Emerson. Please . . ."

Matt was starting to tense up; he looked over at me with confusion and a bit of defensiveness in his eyes. But within myself I felt a dam break — we'd made it through Friday, and Sunday was here. I laughed out loud.

"Matthew, a lot of people love you, and a lot of people are going to help you," I said. "It's simple. We're talking mercy by the numbers. We're going to put your job skills to work and get you out of this mess. I think I've got it figured out. And some parts of the plan are even legal."

I was feeling pretty charitable toward a guy who'd just socked me in the nose. If truth be told, I was a bloody mess once again. Again the injury was minor, but still annoying. My shirt was a little bloody, but I ignored it. It was time to make a few telephone calls.

"First, we need to shore up our defenses before we make the assault," I said. "Can I use your telephone?"

Julie handed me the cordless phone from beside the couch. I dialed Aldridge's number.

"You messed up, preacher," I said when he answered. This time he really was asleep. It was after 11:30. "You broke the rules of pastor-parishioner confidentiality, Mr. Aldridge. I don't guess you can be disbarred for that, but let me explain what it's done. It's torn your church apart."

"What are you talking about?" he asked angrily.

"Julie Robbins. She came to you when she was in pain, and she trusted you. You destroyed that confidentiality by telling Burson. That's why Matt's in trouble now."

"I didn't know he was . . ."

"Yeah, I know. But you've got to help set things straight. I want you to talk to the deacons and steal any thunder Burson might think he has. Tell them it happened a long time ago, that you counseled Julie, and that she's fine now. And then you point out to them — each one of them — that they fall short, too. I don't want any delayed stonings at your church."

"I had no idea . . ."

"Listen, Ed," I said. It was the first time I'd ever called him Ed and not immediately taken it back. "Don't dwell on the mistake. Work on the healing."

I hung up and looked at Matt.

"Matt, how familiar are you with Burson's books?"

"Not very."

"But you're good. If Burson's money man disappeared, would he call you?"

"Maybe . . . Yeah . . . He trusts me. He thinks I'll do whatever he says. Is Freid going to disappear?"

"Watch him," I said. "I need to make one more telephone call."

I dialed a number I knew by heart. When Detective Sergeant Bill Singer answered the phone, I told him I was paying him back for all the times he'd helped me.

"Yeah? How?"

"I'm sending you a federal fugitive from justice," I said. "Be at your local Texas National Bank at, say, 11:45 tomorrow morning. He'll walk straight into your arms. His name is Freid."

"You're making me get up earlier than I usually do on a Saturday," Singer said. "I hope you don't let me down."

"Trust me," I said.

I hung up and looked at David. "Let's go," I said. "We've got some false information to disseminate."

"Is that like lying?" he asked.

"A little . . . Not much . . . Okay . . . I'll talk to Martin about it when we get home."

I told Matt my plan, and he agreed. David and I left and drove toward Freid's home; I'd followed him there a few days before and, amazingly, still remembered the way. It was 12:30 when we knocked on his door. A light came on, and he answered, wearing a robe. He recognized David and squinted at me. I think he slowly realized I was the one who had been his tail for a couple of days.

"What do you want?" he asked.

"You know me?" David said.

"Yes. You work for us. What are you doing here?"

"My name is David Ben Zadok. I don't work for you. But I can work *with* you. You and I are Jews. You should listen to a fellow Jew."

"I'm listening."

"Not out here."

Freid nodded; we went in. He had a nice house, much more assuming on the inside than it was on the outside. He didn't want to display his ill-gotten gain, but he sure wanted to enjoy it. His entertainment center took up an entire wall. I don't think I could stand to be that entertained. We found seats in his plush living room, and David looked at him and whispered conspiratorily, "Are you single?"

"Yes," Freid said. "I'm here alone."

"Fine. Because you are a Jew, I will tell you this: leave town. Certain parties aren't happy with Mr. Burson."

That part was true. Most people who really knew Willie Burson weren't happy with him.

Freid nodded.

"Do you know which parties I speak of?" David asked.

"Yes."

I spoke up. "That's where I come in, Mr. Freid. Just call me a field researcher for certain parties south of the border. Let me ask you this — we've built how many airstrips this year?"

Freid looked nervous. I didn't bother to make him answer.

"Not enough," I said. "Because almost as soon as they are built, the *federales* know where to find them. Is your boss double-dipping, as they say?"

"What do you mean?"

"Is Burson building the airfields and then telling the Feds where to find them?"

"I don't know anything about that. This is the first I've heard . . ."

"Fine. I believe you. If I didn't believe you . . . well, you know what our friends south of the border are like."

I was really starting to enjoy myself.

"What does this mean to me?"

"This means we're giving you a chance to redeem yourself," I said. "We are taking Burson down. Soon. If you want to get out of the way, you must do exactly what I say."

Freid nodded, then looked to David for support.

"First," I said, "you must go to the bank tomorrow morning. Our employers feel they're entitled to a small refund. How much is in Burson's account?"

"As of 5 P.M. Friday, after payroll, just over $128,000," Freid said.

"You should remove all $128,000 — and spare change — as a sign to our employers of your good faith. Then I want you to fly to Houston's Hobby Airport. You'll have just enough time to rent a car and drive to a little town outside Houston. You must get there by noon, before the Texas National Bank there closes. You are to take a deposit slip we give you and the money and deposit the money in that bank. A man, a tall man with a mustache, who is using the name Singer, will be there to meet you. Can you do this?"

Freid appeared a little suspicious. I decided to push him a little further.

"Mr. Freid, please consider this carefully. You've met with other representatives from my employers." I sincerely hoped he had, and I hoped they were intimidating sorts of people. "Those aren't the kind of men who are going to forget you. If you stay here, you will go down with Burson. I'll tell you now, it won't be pretty."

"Hmmph."

"Or you can take the money and leave, try to disappear. But do not be fooled; my employers don't see this as a monetary loss. This is a threat to their authority. You know how they are about *machismo*. They will find you and exact revenge."

Exact revenge? I was starting to embarrass myself. But Freid was evidently buying it. He was getting paler and paler.

"How do I know I can trust you?"

David looked at him, exuding sincerity. "I guarantee you will be treated fairly," he said.

"And if I agree?"

"You will be meeting Singer in a very public place, with security guards and everything. If you get nervous, you can just walk out. He can't just grab you or shoot you."

Of course, he could do both if his little heart was set on it, but I didn't tell Freid that.

"All right. As a sign of my good faith, that I had nothing to do with this . . . with this problem, I will do as you say."

"Good. Be at the bank when it opens and fly immediately to Houston. It's a one-hour flight, and it will take you another hour to rent a car, then get to the Texas National Bank. Be there by noon or they'll start looking for you."

I drew him a map from Hobby Airport to our quaint little town and to the bank David and I both use. "David, a deposit slip, please."

David grinned and pulled out his wallet. He found a deposit slip for his checking account and handed it to Freid.

"Not a word to Mr. Burson now or you'll face the same retribution he will," David said. Retribution. I suppressed a giggle.

Freid actually thanked us as we left.

"What will we do if he doesn't show up at the bank?" David asked.

"It won't matter," I said. "All we really needed was to get him away from the books. I think we've done that. I think now, with one telephone call in the morning, we can start watching the walls crumble."

13

At 8:45 the next morning we were at a pay telephone near the bank that was listed on David's paycheck. We had just seen Freid walk in at 8:30 sharp and walk out fifteen minutes later. He looked nervous. He got into his car and left. We then called Linda Chapman, the federal prosecutor. We'd gotten her number from Julie's father. We told Chapman what was going on. She laughed and said she'd go to her office and work on it. David dialed Burson's home telephone number.

"Mr. Burson?" he said. "This is David Ben Zadok. What? . . . No, I'm calling from the bank . . . No, sir. I went to cash my paycheck, sir, and they told me there was no money in the account. They said Mr. Freid had just come by and taken all the money out."

A pause. "Yes, sir . . . I don't know, sir. He might. I don't know why, they wouldn't tell me. But I thought you should know . . . No, it's not the money. I'm fine. I was just worried about your account . . . Yes, sir. Thank you. Well, I appreciate what you do for me, too . . . Yes, sir. Thanks. Good-bye."

David hung up and smiled. "He'll be here within ten minutes, I bet. He's furious. He asked if I thought the Jew would rip him off. I didn't ask which Jew. Do you think he'll call the cops?"

"Yeah. It would look suspicious if he doesn't."

I pulled out a telephone credit card, dialed the code, and dialed Singer's number.

"I think the pigeon is heading your way," I said.

"Where did you learn to talk, Dunn? Gangster movies and spy flicks? The pigeon? I wonder if I can arrest you for having an awful vocabulary."

"Just arrest this guy, okay? He's going to try to deposit $128,000 into David's account."

David spoke up. "Don't arrest him until after he's through, please."

I elbowed him.

"What am I going to hold him on?" Singer asked. "Your word?"

"Call the U.S. attorney's office in Dallas and talk to Linda Chapman. She's working on this case. She'll be in her office in an hour or so."

I gave him the number. "By the way, Singer, he thinks you're a go-between for some drug smugglers. So dress up a little."

"Thanks for the fashion tip, Mr. Armani," he said. "This could turn into an interesting weekend, Dunn. I almost feel friendly toward you and your partner. Almost."

"We miss you, too, hon. Gotta go now."

I hung up. We waited in David's car in the parking lot for a few minutes until we saw Burson's car drive up. I sank down low in my seat while David got out and approached Burson. They spoke for a few moments; then Burson turned to enter the bank. David came back to the car.

"Did you tell him?" I asked.

"I told him that when I was getting my check on Friday, I saw Mr. Freid take some pages from the accounts books and put them in his briefcase. That was a lie, Emerson."

"I know. I'm sorry. But look at it this way — remember when King David faked insanity when he was hiding out? This is kind of like that, or maybe more like an undercover sting operation.

This is how we're going to bring Burson to justice. See, now he's going to be worried about his money and the books."

"I guess so."

"Look, I'm not so sure about the rightness of all this either. I just figure we've got to do what we can. Now let's go and see our buddy Matt."

We drove to Julie's apartment. Matt had said he would forward his telephone to her place and we could wait there. We found Matt with Julie and Danny; they were eating donuts. They saved us two. One each. I grumbled about being unappreciated as we waited for the call.

This was the weakest link in our chain of hoped-for events. We knew we could make Freid take flight (there's that pigeon again — maybe I *should* cut down on my intake of gangster movies), and we knew we could get Burson all worked up over it. Now it came down to whether Burson would call Matt.

But within an hour he did.

"That's terrible," Matt said into the phone. "Yes, sir . . . Sure. I'll be there first thing Monday morning."

Matt hung up and smiled. "He's worried. He said his accountant ran off with all the ready cash, and he's concerned about his other accounts and investments. He wants me to come in and go over his books."

"That's good, but not very smart," David speculated. "He must know that you think you're going to jail because of him."

"He thinks he owns me," Matt said. "I told him before that I'd die before I'd let Julie get hurt. And he still tries to act like my friend; he assures me that if I get convicted, I'll only get probation."

"Right," I said. "Only you're not going to be convicted. We're going to hand Burson over to the Feds. Now for the next step."

I called our mutual and funky friend Pete and arranged a meeting that afternoon at Levitz's New York Deli. Pete said he'd call Rachel Cohen; he said she knew more about sound than he did, but probably not as much as Danny.

Things were coming together. For us, that is. The Rangers take the lead in the bottom of the first inning.

I called Doug Chen at the Dallas newspaper; I said I'd have 1,200 words to him by Monday night. I outlined the story; he was pleased. He asked about art. I said we'd get mugs of all the principal players.

One last call to Linda Chapman, whom I was starting to like.

"Chapman," she answered.

"This is Emerson Dunn," I said. "We're on. Burson has asked Matt to go in and examine his books Monday morning. He's worried that Freid might have messed with his other investments."

"Good. For your boy to walk, we're going to need some solid stuff."

"We'll go in with a wire," I said. "Matt will lead Burson into explanations about the accounts, if he can. Matt will say he has to know what each account is and where the money goes in order to assess Freid's damage. Burson trusts Matt, so I don't think that will be a problem. I don't think we'll be able to go so far as to get photocopies of the books, though."

"You don't need to. The verbal will do. We'll seize the books Monday night if you come through. I'm getting the warrants ready now."

"Will Matt have to testify?"

Chapman paused. "Maybe. Probably not. That's not how this is going to work."

I wasn't quite sure what she meant, but then I'm no expert at federal investigations. All I knew was that we had a chance to exonerate Matt.

"Thanks. Did you get a warrant for Freid?"

"Your city cop will hold him for questioning long enough for me to get something. You know, that wasn't a bad move. Freid wouldn't have cracked under normal conditions. Now, though,

I think he'll work with us. It must be unsettling to have two lunatics send you down to South Texas with a briefcase full of money, straight into the waiting arms of their policeman friend."

"Thanks for the compliment, I think."

I hung up and leaned back in my chair. Danny, Matt, Julie, and David were looking at me. I grinned. "It's working. I love this country."

Danny threw a throw pillow at me. The tension of Matt's looming indictment was gone, and we could all feel the absence of dread. For the first time since I'd seen him the week before, Matt was starting to look happy. He sat on the couch next to Julie and looked perfect there. I thought about Remington. I thought about jewelry.

14

O f course, things never go as smoothly as we hope. Chaos has been the order of the world since that unfortunate incident with the Tree of Life. Consequently, my plan — such as it was — was destined to meet an unforeseen obstacle or two, something unpredictable. I knew that at the outset — it's always best to plan for the unplannable. And since that makes no sense whatsoever, I figured the best thing to do was to have someone equally unpredictable along — David Ben Zadok.

Over bagels and mid-afternoon coffee, we talked about how things were supposed to go. David, Pete, Danny, Matt, Julie, Rachel Cohen, and I discussed placement, reception, recording devices, and a big blue ugly van. The big blue ugly van belonged to Pete. He carried his drums in it, along with whatever else could be found lurking in the back of it. On Monday it would have Danny and me inside, along with as much recording equipment as we could get our hands on.

Danny pledged to snag us a wireless lapel microphone from his church; we wouldn't need it more than a day. Danny assured us he could tape not only the microphone but also the wireless sending unit to Matt's body in a reasonably undetectable manner.

The wireless receiving unit would be in the van. If we parked as close to the office as possible, we should be able to pick up the signal and record Matt's conversations. Rachel and Danny discussed what equipment they'd need; Rachel had a mixing board she said could filter out most of the background noise and interference. She and Danny would set it all up in the van on Sunday; they would also hook up a monitor so we could hear everything, along with a nice, top-notch cassette recorder. The recorder had a high-speed duplication option on it, she said. The quality of the duplicates wouldn't be great, but they would be passable.

The afternoon crowd at Levitz's Deli was light; no one was around to hear us concoct our plan. Had they been, they might have noticed that David was less than thrilled with the results.

It took me about an hour to realize that myself. David was more quiet than usual. He was next to me at our large round table. I leaned over. "What's wrong?" I asked.

"I feel funny about this," he said. "We'll get the evidence, but how does the prosecutor know this?"

"I don't understand," I said.

"Why didn't *they* set this up? Why didn't they give us the microphones and sit in their own van outside with a tape recorder?"

"I don't know. I guess the deal is they want us to hand them Burson without them having to do anything. Maybe that will make Matt look better."

"Maybe. But I'm still worried. Something isn't kosher."

"Well, that's not a bad frame of mind to be in," I said. "Keeps you on your guard. Maybe you're right."

"I want to be in the van."

"Okay," I said. "I wanted you there anyway."

David nodded; we went back to plotting. An hour later we had it all as planned out as it could get. Pete and Rachel would meet us at Danny's apartment Sunday afternoon; we'd hook up the sound equipment then. Matt would meet us at Danny's at about 7 A.M. Monday. We'd wire him then. And we'd follow him to Burson International, Inc., for a morning of crime-fighting and wrong-righting. By Monday night we would hand-deliver a tape to Chapman, and it would all be over.

Danny, David, and I drove back to Danny's apartment. I called Singer as soon as we got in.

"Did you capture the villain?" I asked when he answered at his office.

"That's it, Dunn. No more Perry Mason reruns for you, young man. Yes, we got him. He's an interesting character. He was almost relieved we were cops instead of Colombians. This guy's confused. The FBI sent a couple of suits down from Houston to pick him up; he's been gone about twenty minutes."

"Great," I said. "How's the chief feel about his detective sergeant helping out on a big federal investigation?"

"He'd rather I find out who has been knocking over the garbage cans in front of Mrs. Donegall's house. She's called him at 7:00 every morning this week."

"Well, as soon as we solve this crime and put away the crook, we'll be right down to help you on that one."

"Oh, would you?"

He was still laughing when I hung up. David was at the kitchen table, writing a letter. It was in Hebrew, so I had no idea what it said.

"Who is that to?" I asked.

"Gershom's father," he said. "I might as well make use of my time. I'm telling him about our time in the army. Gershom didn't talk to his father about it much."

"You don't talk about it much either."

David didn't respond; we'd had this conversation before. It was becoming a stumbling-block in his relationship with Ruth. But it was little use talking to David when he didn't want to discuss something. I left it alone for now.

Danny was on his couch. I went and sat beside him.

"Danny, what happens when Matt is clear?"

"I guess they get married," he said. "Did you know the wedding is all planned?"

"No, I didn't. Is it soon?"

"December, I think."

"Julie always did want a December wedding; right around Christmas. I never knew why. Speaking of Julie, I guess we'd better call A. Vernon Robbins and tell him what has and will transpire."

We called A. Vernon at his home. After about a half-hour's worth of dialogue, he agreed this was our best and probably only hope at getting Matt off the hook.

The last call I made was to Robert. I told him I'd be back Tuesday night or Wednesday. He said they were getting along fine without me. I told him he was pushing it.

That night I made a pot roast, and we watched an old Humphrey Bogart movie on television. It was *To Have or Have Not*, his first with Lauren Bacall. I tried not to think about Remington. I bet she knew how to whistle, though.

There was little to do but wait. David didn't say much during the evening, not even when Bacall taught Bogie to put his lips together and blow.

On Sunday morning David slept in while Danny and I went to church. Getting David to church twice in a row was probably asking a little much from him, considering it wasn't even his religion. I watched for Matt or Julie or even A. Vernon Robbins; I didn't see them.

We drove through a cheap Tex-Mex fast-food place for lunch; we were back at Danny's apartment by 1:00. The others were scheduled to show up at 3:00. For two hours we ate, talked some about tomorrow's plans, and waited.

At 2:45 Pete and Rachel arrived with his van. We went out to the parking lot and helped him stuff the contents of the van into a small corner of it so we'd have room for everything else.

Rachel had the promised cassette recorder, the small monitor, and the mixing board. Danny had the wireless mike he'd borrowed from the church.

We set up the sound system in Pete's van — on Danny's coffee table, which David and I had borrowed for this purpose. The table took up about half of the width of the van and ran from the back of the passenger's seat to within eight inches of the rear door. We had some stadium cushions next to the table; we would sit on them as we listened to Matt and Burson.

Power was the main problem. The mixing board and tape recorder needed 120 volts. We had a small gasoline generator Rachel brought from somewhere, but if we ran it inside the van, it would gas us. We could run it outside the van and run the cord in through the back, but that might be a little suspicious. If we were close enough to Burson's office to pick up the weak signal from the microphone, we'd be close enough for him to wonder what a parked van was doing with a generator running beside it. How do real spies deal with these sorts of problems?

I wasn't happy with the power situation. While Danny and Rachel and Pete worked out the bugs in the mike and receiver and recorder, I said I'd like to go survey the office area again. David said he'd go with me.

We drove north to Burson International, Inc. and looked over the scene — the office, one in a series of offices in the small complex, the pizza joint across the street, and the rest. There were no cars in the parking lot in front of Burson; we parked there and got out.

The complex consisted of a number of offices in a nice, understated brick building. The wood trim was stained, not painted, and there were shrubs in front, providing a visual buffer between the complex and the busy street. There were four companies spaced out in the six offices; two offices were unoccupied. The office on the far left belonged to a chiropractor, the next office to a software company; the next one was vacant, and the one after that was Burson. To the right of Burson was a temporary personnel agency, and the office on the far right was empty.

And in the shrubs, pointing up at the doors, were small green-based security lights. I noticed them about the same time David did. He walked over to one and knelt.

"Good — just one photoelectric switch," he said, "for the whole bank of lights . . . Over there." He pointed to the first lamp in the series, to our left. It was larger than the others; it had a light-sensing switch on it facing away from the lamp itself.

"It could work," David said. "But it won't be convenient. It will take some effort."

"What do we need to do?"

"We'll need to show up before the sun," he said. "We will use electrical tape to cover the photo cell on the switch; then it will think it's still night, and the lights will stay on. Then we will unscrew all of the lights just a little bit, so they're still in place but not making contact and not lighting up. And then, on the far right, we will remove the bulb and replace it with the kind of electrical outlet you can screw into a light socket. We will bring an extension cord, bury it in the grass next to the shrubbery for about, what, two meters, and park the van on the far end, at the edge of the grass. We will bring the cord under the van, up to the passenger door, on the side away from Burson's office, and *voila*, we have power. It will be visible if you're looking for it, but no more visible than a loud generator."

"I like it. Can we do all that in time?"

"It should take about twenty minutes," David said after a pause. "Two people. You want to help?"

"Sure. I'll wake you at about 5 A.M."

We drove back to the apartment. Matt and Julie were there, along with the others. They were inside, and Matt had his shirt off. Danny was taping the microphone to his chest, in the indention at his solar plexus. With a tie-on, Danny explained, it wouldn't be noticeable. Danny then taped the wire leading from the mike to Matt's side, around to his back. Danny taped the FM sending unit to the small of Matt's back. Danny showed Matt the switch, but after seeing Matt fumbling with it at his back, we decided it would be best to turn it on before he went into the office.

Danny and Rachel and Pete went out to the van to test the strength of the signal. They had strung an extension cord from Danny's apartment to the van. If the signal could make it through the apartment's walls and door to the parking lot, it could reach from inside Burson's office to where we would be in the van. Matt and Julie talked in normal voices for a while, and in a few minutes Danny entered with a smile. It picked up clear as a bell, he said.

I ordered a pizza, which we ate as we went over the final plans. After another two hours, everyone else went home.

Danny, David, and I barely slept that night. I wanted to talk about variables, about what could go wrong at each stage of the plan.

David said I should be quiet and go to sleep. We'd done everything we could to prepare, and we would do more in the morning.

"Besides," he said, "it's in the hands of God."

"I've noticed that we tend to say that mainly when we doubt the ability of our own hands," I said. "I wonder how God feels about that. He probably doesn't like it."

"You're being cynical."

"I guess you're right," I said. "Well, let's stop worrying and get some sleep."

"I've been saying that for two hours now."

"You're right, David. I should listen to you more often. Go to sleep. It's after 1 A.M."

A little more than four hours later, David and I were in his

Toyota, pulling into the still-dark parking lot of Burson International. The street in front was almost deserted. If we were quick, we could get the job done without trying to explain our motives to an attentive cop. We parked and immediately went to work. He had some gaffer's tape, which he used to cover the light sensor on the first security lamp. The lamps would stay on now. I had some of Danny's pot-holders — ones I recognized from our days of rooming together — and I starting unscrewing the lights just enough to where they'd go dark. When I got to the last one, David was waiting for me.

I unscrewed the lamp completely, and he quickly screwed in a regular 120-volt outlet. He had a heavy-duty black extension cord, which he plugged into the socket, then laid out snake-like along the ground for about seven feet to the end of the grass. We decided that the cable was inconspicuous enough to lay along the edge of the grass, right where the concrete started, without being noticed. You could see it, but only if you were looking for it. I wasn't worried. People generally see what they expect to see, and it's amazing how much they overlook if the setting is familiar.

It took us a little more than fifteen minutes in all. We were back in the car and on the road toward Danny's by 5:45. Danny was awake and showered by the time we got back. Matt arrived at 7:15, a few minutes ahead of Pete. Pete dropped off his van, took Matt's car, and said good luck. I said we hoped we wouldn't need any.

At 8:30 Matt was wired for sound. All batteries had been replaced with new ones, all connections had been checked, and all systems were go. We piled into the van, with Matt in front and David, Danny, and I in the back. We drove into the parking lot a few minutes before 9:00, but there were already cars in front of Burson International, including Burson's car, the Cadillac.

Danny said a quick prayer out loud as we parked at the far

right end of the building. Matt took a deep breath, then got out and strolled slowly and calmly down the walkway to Burson's office. When the office door closed behind him, David hopped out on the passenger's side, grabbed the power cord, and brought it back into the van. We shut the door on it, then used a shorter extension cord with multiple outlets to hook up the equipment. The indecipherable lights and meters came on, and through the monitors we could hear Matt talking to someone.

"Sure, which accounts do you want me to look at?"

"The books are over there." It was clearly Burson's voice. He sounded nervous.

I nodded at Danny. He hit a button, and the cassette tape started recording.

A few minutes of silence went by. We heard a muffled whispery sound, as if Matt were flipping through pages of a ledger book.

"Mr. Burson, this account here . . . What is it?"

"That's not important. Just go over the numbers."

"The monies in these accounts keep moving, Mr. Burson. I need to know where the money comes from and where it's supposed to go if I'm going to tell you if any has been stolen."

Another pause. "Okay. Belize Petrochemical and Development — the one there, at the top . . . That's where you wire the money from the church."

"I wired that money to a missions group."

"You know better than that. It's the same account. Belize Petrochemical and Development pays a consultant's fee every month. To me. My personal account. Over here, on this page."

It went on like that for about two hours. They tracked money through offshore accounts, through bogus enterprises, and even through a few respectable investment firms.

Burson laughed when Matt got to a column filled with debits. "Those are my county projects," Burson said. "I'm giving a little back to the community. I lose thousands per week sometimes on these projects, but it's good public relations. I can afford it."

By 11:00 it was getting stuffy in the van, even with the windows down. So far no one had noticed us. We flipped the tape over every half-hour and changed it every hour. We weren't comfortable but we were getting good stuff. Burson outlined several methods he used to launder money; he was personally making about $500,000 per year building his rural runways, he said. That was net.

Last year $200,000 of that had been laundered by the church — he'd even gotten a tax deduction for his efforts. Another $155,000 was washed through a South American bank; it returned to him as capital gains on investments in Venezuela. He had to pay taxes on that, he complained to Matt. The remaining $145,000 went to cover what he lost doing business with the government.

"Freid was doing a good job for you," Matt admired.

"Sure was. But now he's gone. Don't you worry, I'll find him. But with you here, I don't need him. Maybe I'll give him a chance to return my money, or maybe I won't."

By a quarter to noon it was all over. Matt's signal was fading; we'd gotten all we needed, and we wanted to get the van out of the parking lot before the lunch crowd started emerging from the various offices. It was time for our signal. David got out of the van and went into the office. Since he was still a trusted member of Burson International, he walked in calmly. He was there to pick up the tax forms he hadn't filled out yet, he told the secretary.

On the monitor we heard Matt tell Burson he was going to get some lunch. Burson said they could meet back at the office at 1 P.M. Matt agreed. Matt walked out of the building a few steps in front of David. Matt got in on the driver's side; David paused long enough to unplug the extension cord and toss it out onto the pavement. Matt started to back the van out, but David said to wait.

A moment later David had his Nikon out, and he snapped off three shots of Burson as he walked out of the office building. He shot over Matt's shoulder, and the window was rolled up, so Burson didn't see him.

"Finished," he said. Matt put the van into reverse, and we backed out.

Two blocks later I started breathing again. I grabbed one of the tapes and stuck it into the cassette player in the van's dashboard. It was clear and true. I smiled and told Matt to drive to A. Vernon's office.

"You call him that too?" he asked.

"Yeah. Always have. He ignores it," I said.

"What's the A. stand for?"

"I have no idea. I never found out."

Within a few minutes all four of us sat in front of A. Vernon Robbins. We handed him the tapes as he punched the intercom and asked Pearl to get Linda Chapman on the telephone.

"She's on line 1," Pearl's voice said a minute later.

A. Vernon picked up the phone and grinned. "We've got three hours' worth of tape," he said. "All of it juicy. Do you want to hear it?"

He paused. "Good. We'll see you in an hour."

He hung up and looked at us. "She's on her way here."

I asked if I could borrow a computer for a while. A. Vernon agreed. He kicked a secretary off hers and told me to use it as long as I needed to. I'd been making notes during our short stint as a mobile recording studio, and I was ready to crank out an article. I had 1,252 words within an hour and a half. I was starting to read over it for the second time when Linda Chapman walked into the office, about forty-five minutes late.

"Good afternoon, Mr. Dunn," she said as I stood to accompany her into A. Vernon's office. She was smiling and wearing a white linen suit. Her dark hair was up in a bun. She looked like someone's idea of a woman prosecutor.

"I rank as Mr. Dunn now? Are you this formal with all your federal witnesses?"

"Who said you would be a witness?"

She said nothing more as she walked into A. Vernon's chambers. "Do you have the tapes?" she said.

Danny produced the three numbered cassettes — her copies, though we had made copies for ourselves. I'd need them as documentation for my article.

Chapman pulled a small tape player from her briefcase. She inserted the first tape, and we listened to about five minutes of it. She removed the tape without rewinding it, then put in the third tape. She listened for maybe two minutes.

"These will do nicely," she said. "Mr. Hall, the charges will be dropped. You never met any of Mr. Burson's business associates, did you?"

"Me? No," Matt said. "I just did as I was told."

"Well then . . . Thank you. This was good work." She stood to leave.

"That's it?" I asked.

"Is there something more, Mr. Dunn?"

"Well, I don't know," I said after a moment. "I guess not. But this seems kind of unceremonious."

"You gave me the tapes, and your friend goes free. I think that's enough ceremony. Mr. Robbins can take care of the details with the court clerk in the morning."

I was a little confused. Chapman wasn't elated, she wasn't dejected, she wasn't pensive, she wasn't even very appreciative. Nailing a high-profile crook like Burson should have made her at least a little excited; it was the sort of bust that can make a career. But it seemed to be just another day at work for her.

She left after a few pleasantries. Yes, yes, she'd be in touch, she said. And by the way, we weren't to speak of this matter to anyone, especially the press.

I said nothing.

When she was out of the office, David turned to me. "What did she mean by that?"

"Lamps and bushels, David. Lamps and bushels."

15

We didn't know what had gone wrong until 5:30 P.M. when we got a call from Rev. Ed Aldridge. We'd been at Danny's for a couple of hours, after dropping off the article and film with Doug Chen.

"Emerson, could you and Matthew come by my office? There are some things we need to go over."

"Sure," I said. "Now?" I had just taken a shower.

"Yes . . . Please."

Aldridge sounded insistent, but not desperate. I said we'd be there in half an hour. Maybe he was having second thoughts about talking with the deacons about Julie. Matt was still waiting for Pete to come by and pick up his van (and give Matt back his car). I told Matt that Aldridge wanted to see us, and he nodded.

"Why?" David asked as we started for the door.

"Dunno," I said. "He just wants to see us."

Matt and I drove my car to the church. When we got there I suddenly realized that there were problems in my life. Burson's Caddy was parked next to Aldridge's car. Matt didn't say anything.

We stayed in the car for a moment. I started to put the car in reverse and back out when I felt Matt's hand on my shoulder.

"No," he said. "It's about Julie. We've got to see what he wants."

I nodded and turned off the car. We walked into the church and around to the office. Burson was there with Aldridge. Burson looked angry; Aldridge looked nervous.

"What did you think you were going to pull, Matt?" Burson asked. "Did you think you could beat me? After all these years, all the punks like you . . ."

Burson was standing, leaning against one of Aldridge's bookcases. His arms were crossed; he looked at Matt.

"You've blown it, Matt. You too." He looked over at me. "Ed tells me you're a friend of Matt's. He says you used to date Julie, that little slut. You the one who knocked her up?"

Matt started to protest, but Burson advanced and threw a backhand punch that caught Matt in the face. He followed it with a strong right to Matt's stomach. Matt grabbed the edge of Aldridge's desk for support. Aldridge, sitting eighteen inches from his parishioner, turned away so he wouldn't have to look at Matt. Burson hadn't expended much effort and resumed his pose against the bookcase.

I was still near the doorway. Burson looked at me questioningly. "You want some too?"

"Getting a little old for boxing, aren't you?" I asked.

Burson shrugged. It was then I heard soft footsteps out in the hallway. Burson looked over my shoulder and frowned.

"David?" he said.

"Hello, Mr. Burson," David said cheerily.

Burson looked confused. David stepped in beside me. "I was right; this time I trusted my instincts," he said to me. "I thought I'd better follow you guys over here. That lady lawyer didn't want the tapes for evidence, Emerson. That's why she didn't care about the quality and why she wasn't so excited to get them. She only wanted them as leverage. You know how they didn't really want Matt? They don't really want Burson either.

They want him to tell who his contacts are, I bet. Nobody ever gets punished as long as they rat on the next level. In Israel, it is the same way."

Burson was starting to put things together. David wasn't on his side. Burson, all 6-feet-2 of him, went from his leaning posture to a closed, attentive stance. His arms were still folded but ready. "You're with them? That's fine. We're just going to establish who's who around here."

"And Singer says *I* watch too many movies," I said. "Matt, are you going to live?"

Matt was still leaning on the desk. He nodded. He probably couldn't talk yet. An awful lot of wind got knocked out of him with that right.

"Aldridge, act like a pastor and help Matt to a chair," I said.

"Stay there, Ed," Burson said. "I'm in charge here."

"Who was it who said that when Reagan got shot?" I asked David. "Ed, don't pay any attention to him. Take care of Matt."

Aldridge stayed put. I was hoping he could get Matt to a chair or out of the room before the inevitable showdown started. But maybe things weren't so inevitable.

"You think you've won, right?" I said to Burson.

"Won? Son, I own the game. I just have to name a few names, and I even get to keep the money I've made. If I work things right, they'll let me keep building the airfields so they'll have a reliable informant inside this end of the cartel. And you boys are going to crawl under some rock after this fight is over, if you're able to."

"Lamps and bushels, Mr. Burson. Lamps and bushels."

"What are you talking about, son?"

"Well, sir," I said, drawling it out a little so Burson could understand me, "didn't you go to Sunday school? When you light a lamp, you don't hide it under a bushel basket. The truth wasn't meant to be hidden. On the front page of tomorrow's

Dallas paper there's a 1,250-word story written by yours truly. It's all about you and your exploits."

Burson looked a little nervous. "Your friends . . . they're in this too. They'd be hurt."

"Like I said, the truth wasn't made to be hidden. It's all in there. Including Matt's deal with the Feds — they won't go back on that deal now, Burson. And I included as many details as I could about your money laundering. So the prosecutor is going to have to either rethink her deal to you or rethink her career. If there's one thing this administration hates, it's bad PR. And letting a guy like you walk, after the whole world knows what you've done, is about as bad as PR gets."

He came across the room at me and threw a punch that would have knocked me halfway into tomorrow. Instead, my friend David knocked me merely into another time zone with an elbow. I went down, and David went forward.

David deflected the punch with his forearm and sent a pretty nice kick into Burson's left knee. Burson gurgled and fell.

David helped me up as Burson lay holding his leg. There were tears in Burson's eyes.

"He told me about that knee," David said. "Old construction accident. That's a shame."

"Glad you tagged along, David. Remember to always trust your instincts."

He nodded. Matt was recovering and looked a little less red. He was staring down at Burson. Aldridge was, too.

"Reverend, I think the time has come for your resignation," I said. He didn't look up at me.

"I didn't know Burson was going to . . ."

"You knew. You at least suspected. But you refused to do what was right."

He stared down at his desk. I shook my head. "Matt, let's go. Mr. Aldridge, it's called complicity. You're guilty. You know what you have to do. You've had trouble in the past doing what's right, so let me warn you — if you don't step down, this is going in the newspaper also."

It didn't feel good, bullying a preacher. I have too much respect for most of them to begrudge them their humanity. But this was different.

Without any help, Matt followed David and me out the door. Burson hadn't moved. Aldridge was getting up to help him as we left.

Once outside, I turned to Matt. "Drive my car home," I said. "I need to talk to David."

Matt looked at my car, the sky-blue land-whale I affectionately call an automobile.

He nodded and took my keys. What a guy. I followed David to his car; we got in and started toward Danny's.

"Good call," I said. "You were right about the deal not being kosher."

He gave me a sideways glance.

"I should listen to you more often," I said. "But this doesn't really change anything. This doesn't make up for Gershom."

"I know. I can't change that. But I can change myself, I guess. I have good instincts. I can pay more attention to them."

I waited. I could sense that he wanted to continue talking, to maybe work something out inside himself.

"I only hurt Mr. Burson as much as I had to," David said. "And I only hurt you as much as I had to. But I have hurt a lot of people."

I nodded, still not saying anything.

"The thing is, I don't know what to do about it. What would you do, Emerson?"

"Are you sure this is about other people — or is it about you? Where's the pain right now?"

"Inside."

"Right. I think you have to fix that first. There's such a thing as mercy, David. I've seen a lot of it. I expect I'll see plenty more before all is said and done. And believe me, there's plenty enough for you. That's why Jesus died."

"That's hard for me, Emerson."

"I know, and I won't push it. But realize this — I'm nothing without that mercy. Matt would be nothing without mercy either. All we did was accept it. I've heard people from both our faiths say that the God of the Jews and the God of the Christians are different. I don't think they are. I think you know the God I'm talking about. The God who heard Israel's moaning in Egypt is the same God who brought Matt and me out of our own kinds of slavery. When you're ready, David, He's there. I can help show you the way."

He nodded but didn't respond verbally. We drove the rest of the way to Danny's apartment without talking. It wasn't an uncomfortable silence, just one I wasn't sure was ready to be broken.

Matt was at Danny's when we arrived; so was Pete. Julie was on her way. So were a few other people, mostly people I didn't know. From the time Linda Chapman had told all within hearing distance that the charges against Matt were being dropped, the word had been spreading. Julie said she'd gotten twenty or twenty-five phone calls, mainly from people in their church. A crowd started gathering at Danny's; by 9:30 the apartment was full.

For the rest of the evening I sat back and watched my friends. Danny had been right; he usually was, come to think of it. I'd been willing to give up on Matt too early. Danny wasn't, and I thought he was just being naive.

Matt spent most of the evening at Julie's side. It wasn't possessive — it was protective. I didn't know how to feel about Julie, but I knew I felt pretty comfortable with the idea of them as a couple.

It was getting late, and I was letting my guard down some when I heard a voice over my shoulder.

"Still watching," Pete said. "You always did watch people."

"You caught me staring?"

"Yeah," he said, sitting on the arm of the chair I was in. The din was loud enough that we could have a private conversation although there were fifteen people in the living room alone.

"You still care for her?" he asked.

"No . . . not like that. Not like he does."

"Didn't think you did."

I nodded. "He's good for her."

"He's good, period. He's way ahead of us in a lot of areas. It used to bother me, but not now. Not after things like what we did today. There are still purposes for the likes of us."

"Yeah, the likes of us," I said after a moment. "If nothing else, we're good at what we do."

"That's just what I was going to say." Pete grinned at me as he stood up. "Keep in touch."

"I will. Keep it funky. You've got to keep the standard high for those of us who are funk-disabled."

"I'll do it. Someone's got to save you from button-down collars, Emerson."

Pete left a few minutes before the telephone rang. Danny called out my name over the rumble of voices. I got up and took the call in his bedroom. I closed the door. It was Doug on the phone.

"Good piece. We ran the film you guys dropped off; you won't need to come down and ID the men if you assure me that Hall is the young guy and Burson is the old guy."

"That's right."

"That's $400 for the story and $100 for the mug shots. That enough?"

"More than enough. Not a bad vacation. And my photographer even got a paycheck from Burson out of the deal."

"Let's talk deals, Dunn. We're going to need to follow this story for a few months — not immediately, but later when the trial starts. For now, our editorial board is writing a piece based on your story; we're going to say it would be a terrible, awful thing to let Burson off. The U.S. attorney for the Southern District — not the assistant you're dealing with, but her boss — is going to hate it."

Doug laughed at that for a moment. "But, Dunn, in a few months I'm going to need a person on this full-time. I'd like for it to be you. You're talented, resourceful, and you're probably cheap."

"Are you proposing to me?"

"I'm offering you a job, Dunn, and for a newspaper that hasn't hired a new writer in ten months, that's a pretty big deal. I want you to come to work for me, beginning January 1st. I know that's a few months away, but that's when my new budget starts, and that's when I'll need you."

"What about my shooter?"

"Package deal? My board liked his role in the investigation. I think they'd go for it. Is he as cheap as you?"

"Probably. You're a charmer, Doug. But I've got to talk this over with David and with some others. Can I call you in a few days?"

"Take your time. But call me."

"I will. And thank you."

I hung up and suddenly found myself feeling very alone in a crowded apartment. Matt's life was going to return to normal. Mine couldn't. Things were changing, and I didn't know what to do about it. A small-town reporter doesn't turn down an offer like that from a major metropolitan newspaper. That's what we work toward; that's the goal. I could get back into writing and away from the adult world of editing; that in itself was attractive.

Doug had even made an offer for David. David would go for it in a minute, I was sure. It would be the smart thing.

But the idea of leaving my comfortable small town was more

than a little frightening. What would Airborne think about leaving the farm so soon?

And there was more. What had Julie said about effort? I hadn't made any effort to get her back, to find out what the problem really was.

I wasn't making much of an effort with Remington, either. She was waiting for me at home, watching my dog. She was still living in town although she was working an hour's drive away — just so she could be closer to me. She was there at my side every Sunday when I faced the masses of junior high school kids.

I picked up the telephone, barely feeling it in my hand. I felt as if I'd just slipped into a strange and confusing dimension in which men tend to overcome jewelry phobias very quickly.

I dialed David's home telephone number. His Uncle Mordechai was staying with David and his family, I knew. Carl, David's stepfather, answered on the first ring. I asked to speak to Mordechai.

"This is Emerson," I said when the old Israeli answered. "Let's talk about jewelry. I'm going to need a ring."

"Hmmm. I think we carry those, yes," Mordechai said after a pause. "Tell me, is this ring for someone special? Your mother perhaps?"

"You know what kind of ring I'm talking about," I said. "You probably even know the size."

"Yes, as a matter of fact. I have examined her hand on several occasions, such as when you dined here, and I knew then that you would become a customer. Size 7."

"So what are we going to do about it?"

"My young friend, you are coming home tomorrow? That is when David said he will be home."

"I'll be there."

"I will have a selection picked out. I have a stone, a marquise diamond, a particularly outstanding one. Not too expensive. But for a love such as yours, I'm sure price is no matter."

For a bank account such as mine, price was a laughing matter. But I didn't say that. I thanked him and hung up.

Then I dialed Martin's number. The kids were in bed already, so he answered the phone. I asked if he was still awake. He said he was. And then we talked for about twenty minutes. I thanked him and hung up.

I dialed my own home number. Maggie answered. I said hello and asked if Remington was available. She said yes, and a moment later Aggie Catherine Remington came to the telephone.

"It's over," I said. "The good guys won."

"I knew you would. What happened?"

I gave her the condensed version. She was impressed. I told her about the front-page story in tomorrow's paper. She was impressed again.

"So what about Julie?"

"What about her?" I asked.

"Is she going to be okay?"

"She's okay with it, I think. It turns out Matt's pride was a factor all along. He's getting better about it. I think that eventually they'll both come to terms with it."

"What about their relationship?"

"Matt's a good man. Good for her, I guess. Better than I was."

"Are they laid to rest, then?"

"Who?" I asked.

"The ghosts . . . The ghosts I sent you to put to rest. Have you done that?"

I closed my eyes. I could almost see Remington. She was probably wearing one of her dad's dress shirts and sweatpants. A strange combination, but for her, fairly common. "The ghosts are gone," I said. "Most of them anyway. I still don't have all the answers for We The Living. In fact, I'm coming up with more and more questions."

"Questions," she said slowly. "Yes, I was wondering when that would come up. Emerson, I've got one more question for you."

I paused. If this was going somewhere, it was somewhere I hadn't intended. "Shoot."

"Emerson, I got a letter today. I've been accepted to law school at Southern Methodist University in Dallas."

My stomach tightened. "I didn't know you had applied."

"I took the law school admissions test when I first got out of college," she said. "And I applied then. I applied again last spring. I never found a way to bring it up without sounding like I'm tired of you . . . of us. I don't want you to think that now. It's just that I've been working at the Houston paper for six months and I'm starting to realize it's not what I want to do forever. But, Emerson, this isn't something that needs to bring about big changes. There are law schools in Houston, ones that would be cheaper than SMU, closer to home. I can apply to them."

I breathed slowly. I find that breathing is essential to making statements such as the one I was about to make.

"Dallas is fine," I said.

"What does that mean — to us?" She said it in a casual manner, sort of like saying, "What's that thing sticking its head out of the washing machine?" in a casual manner.

"Well, Aggie Catherine Remington, it means that we could be on the right track. I got a job offer from Doug at the Dallas paper. Not for immediately. It would start January 1st, when his new budget starts. He's serious, and he wants David, too. What I mean is, can you take tomorrow off?"

"I think so."

"Good. I want to do a little shopping. I'll be there by noon."